DESTINY'S TWINS

You are so there.

T*WITCHES

T·WITCHES

**H.B. GILMOUR
& RANDI REISFELD**

SCHOLASTIC INC.
NEW YORK   TORONTO   LONDON   AUCKLAND   SYDNEY
MEXICO CITY   NEW DELHI   HONG KONG   BUENOS AIRES

ISBN 0-439-49232-7

12 11 10 9 8 7 6 5 4 3 2 1   4 5 6 7 8 9/0

PRINTED IN THE U.S.A.   40
FIRST PRINTING, FEBRUARY 2004

DEDICATION

For Jess, as always, with love.
—H.B.G.

To SR, SR & MR, with love always.
—R.R.

The authors would like to give a special shout-out to
Aimee Friedman, who used her own good magick to
help and heal when it was most needed.

CHAPTER ONE
BETWEEN TWO WORLDS

"I'd rather die." Barefoot and fuming, Alexandra Fielding stalked back and forth across the bedroom she shared with her twin sister, Camryn Barnes.

"Could you *be* more dramatic?" Cam studied her freshly painted toenails. Alex sneered at them.

It was Thursday morning, way too early for a spa moment, in Alex's opinion. She'd awakened fifteen minutes ago knowing something important was going to happen today. Cam's unexpected announcement was so not it.

"You mean could I be less like you?" Alex scoffed, pointing an accusing finger at her twin. "See, that's what I mean —"

"What, that your nails are toxic-dump green and

mine are Perfectly Pink?" Cam removed the foam rubber separators from between her toes and stood up cautiously. "We're talking about a sweet sixteen party, Alex — not some devious form of torture."

"Right, and what I'd really like for my birthday is shame and humiliation. Are you sure you read Emily's mind right?"

Emily was Cam's adoptive mom, an interior designer and petite, blond bundle of energy. Yesterday evening, she'd bustled through the front door with a bouquet of shopping bags from which brightly colored tissue papers peeped. Cam, who was on her way downstairs, had picked up a curious vibe crackling off Emily.

Having visions, clairvoyant peeks into the future, was one of Cam's special gifts. But her mind-reading mojo was nowhere near as sharp as her sister's. Alex had been able to pick brains undetected for years while Cam had only recently found herself able to catch a mumbled thought here, a mind-mutter there. But she'd peered down at her slyly grinning mom and tapped into a gold mine.

Emily was planning a secret sweet sixteen party for them!

Exactly where and when hadn't been decided yet, only that it was going to be a surprise — which meant that it might *not* be held on Halloween, the twins' actual birthday.

Even if Cam hadn't been able to break into her mom's thoughts, the electricity sparking Em's thousand-watt smile would have tipped her off. The woman was glowing with barely contained excitement.

Cam had to admit she'd gotten pretty stoked herself. Her head had instantly whirled with ideas for what she'd wear, who she'd invite, whether the party would be thrown at home — a backyard tent? Or away — if it was all girls, spa sweet sixteens were extremely cool. . . . All she had to do was find a way to let Emily know that her secret was past tense and Cam could so do this party — *her* way.

Monkey wrench? Alex. Especially since Cam had just made the mistake of sharing the news with her joy-squishing twin.

Cam sighed now, regretting her mistake. "Get over yourself, Alex. You're not the only birthday babe around here. I have something to say about it, too. You may not want a major coming-of-age bash, but I do. And, more important, so does Emily. She's been planning this since —"

"Since you were a teeny-weeny little witch?" Alex interrupted. "Excuse me, Camryn, but your mom doesn't have a clue. For starters, she thinks you're normal. Oops, I forgot. Not exactly normal. Emily thinks you're the best thing to happen to civilization since fish grew feet."

Alex flopped down on the floor and leaned her

head back against her bed. It was heaped with a Salvation Army bin's worth of recently worn clothes and a bevy of old leather-bound books. Some of the books had recently been given to the twins by their biological mom, Miranda DuBaer; a few, including *The Little Book of Spells,* had come from their cousin Ileana; the rest were borrowed from the library on Coventry, the witch-populated island where Miranda and Ileana lived, and where Alex and Cam had been born.

Born, but not bred.

From the get-go, Coventry had been deemed too dangerous for them.

Their father had been murdered on the very day of their birth. Their mother had gone mad with grief and been sent far away to recover. And their uncle Thantos, fearing they would one day take his place as head of the powerful DuBaer family, had tried to kidnap them. So the twins had been smuggled off the island as infants and entrusted to separate adoptive families or protectors, never knowing of their true witchy heritage.

At the age of fourteen, Alex, who'd been living with her beloved protector, Sara Fielding, in a tumbledown trailer in Crow Creek, Montana, had, for the first time, laid eyes — intense, metallic-gray eyes — on the twin she'd never known she had, Camryn Barnes of Marble Bay, Massachusetts.

Only then, after years of wondering and worrying, did they both discover what was "wrong" with them. They were witches. Twin witches. T'Witches.

Their word.

On Coventry, they were considered "fledglings" — at least until they completed their Initiation.

The big event — which Cam thought of as their WATs, Witch Aptitude Tests, as opposed to next year's SATs — would finally make them full-fledged witches.

As far as Alex was concerned, their Initiation was way more important than some sappy "sweet" sixteen party crammed with her sister's snobby friends and hangers-on.

Alex grabbed one of the books from her bed and rifled noisily through its pages, to show Cam that she was too busy to care about Emily's lame bender. That finally becoming what they'd been born to be was what *really* counted.

The Initiation was to begin on the first day of their birth month, October, and be completed at the end of the month, with forty-eight hours of tests and ceremonies on Coventry.

On Coventry.

Flash! Alex looked up from her book.

Maybe that was why Cam wasn't all that psyched. Their last trip to the island, a couple of months back, had almost turned deadly. Thanks to their treacherous uncle, the same Thantos DuBaer who'd tried to snatch them as infants, Cam had been lured into a near-lethal trap. And thanks to another young witch in Thantos's service, Alex had almost been sent far away, separated from Cam for good.

The most important thing that had happened, though, had been the discovery that the twins were supposed to take over the dynasty now headed by their devious uncle.

It was, Miranda and Ileana kept saying, their destiny.

Maybe, Alex thought, tossing *The Coventry Catalog of Herbs* back onto the heap of books and laundry on her bed. Then again, maybe not.

What if she didn't want to run a dynasty?

She'd thought about becoming a musician, a songwriter, maybe even a social worker or psychologist, since she dug helping people and, with magick at her disposal, wasn't too shabby at it.

Cam hadn't shared what she'd hoped her future would hold. But Alex couldn't imagine her twin leaving Marble Bay, and her friends, and the adoptive family who'd loved and protected her practically since the day she was born. Although being in command — whether of a dynasty, a soccer team, or Emily's secret blowout — was second nature to her controlling sister.

Whatever became of them, it wouldn't happen until after their Initiation.

Alex turned suddenly and looked at the digital clock on the night table between her bed and Cam's. The time, day, and date shone back at her in electric red.

It was Thursday. Okay, she knew that. They had the day off from school because of a teachers' conference. But that wasn't it. That wasn't why today was so special!

"May I remind you," Alex told her sister, "that we've got more important things to focus on than some lame sweet sixteen party."

Cam tried to glare at her twin. It didn't work. She was suddenly as blue as her toenails were pink. She'd been fighting off sadness and disillusion since their terrifying trip to Coventry.

She had gone to the little island hoping to "save" a handsome young warlock who'd begged for her help. She'd left knowing that he was a fraud, a traitor, and an all-around rat. Shane was his name. Deception was his game.

Cam screwed the cap back on the bottle of nail polish and tossed it into the basket on her bureau. She glanced at her glossy toenails, which now matched her fingertips. Perfectly Pink. It was almost as pathetic an attempt to stoke her mood as the idea of planning her own sweet sixteen party.

"You're the one who doesn't have a clue," she mumbled at Alex. "Has it occurred to you I may not *want* to think about Coventry Island right now? It feels like we just got back. And may I remind *you* the trip was not a piece of cake!"

Even if she didn't have her sister's telescopic eyesight, Alex couldn't help seeing that Cam was miserable. Torn between guilt and sympathy, Alex tried to lighten the atmosphere. "Speaking of cake, I'm gonna grab some breakfast. Come with?" she offered.

New as she was to the mind-reading game, Cam caught her sister's solicitous gist. "Spare me your pity," she grumbled.

"Oh, forget Shane," Alex urged.

Her twin winced at the name. "Thank you, Dr. Phil," she said, trying for indifference.

Alex shook her head in frustration and headed out the door.

"Sorry," Cam called softly — too low and too late, of course. Her sister had already thundered down the stairs.

Duck-walking on the balls of her feet to avoid smearing her hot-pink toenails, Cam made her way over to the clothes hamper that passed for Alex's bed. She was familiar with *The Little Book of Spells* but she picked it up anyway. It had no table of contents, so she began leafing though it . . . looking for? It embarrassed her to admit it, even to herself, but she wondered if she'd find, somewhere in its yellowing pages, a spell to cure what ailed her.

Which was?

Love? Not exactly. More like . . . obsession, she guessed. Not being able to shake the memory and shame of Shane's betrayal, not being able to do exactly what Alex had advised. Forget it. Forget him.

Right — and what, see him again when she and Alex had to go back to Coventry for the final two days of their Initiation?

Cam took a deep breath. Alex had been right. Absolutely. Don't sweat the small stuff, she'd told Cam more than once. And Shane was small stuff. Microscopic compared to the trials and tests that would make them real witches.

What really mattered was their Initiation.

Which was coming up —

Was it possible?! Cam looked at the digital clock. The date glared back at her. OCT OI! The first of October.

Their Initiation had begun!

CHAPTER TWO
THE RULES

On the last day of their last visit to Coventry, Cam remembered, she and Alex had been taken by Miranda and Ileana to an imposing cottage at the east end of the island. The pebbled path to its door wound through herbs and flowers so lush that they towered over the twins.

Inside, surrounded by bowls of glittering crystals and stones, ancient books on the craft, and jars of potions and lotions of every kind and color, Lady Rhianna lived. She, Ileana had informed them, was to be their Initiation Master. There and then, she would explain the rules of their upcoming Initiation.

As Rhianna came forward to greet them, the plus-size witch's broad hips and folded wings brushed against the shelves and tables holding her remarkable collections.

She hadn't invited them to sit down. There was no place for that, anyway. There were few pieces of furniture, chairs included, that weren't overflowing with herb jars, books, or display boxes. Sparing the small talk, she began.

"It is the tradition of this community that rites of Initiation be given when fledglings come of age. It is an event that will unfold over the course of one full month —"

Event, right. The large in-charge witch could call it anything she wanted, Cam thought now, but it was essentially a test. An evaluation. An exam. They could pass it . . . or they could fail. She'd realized that minutes after Rhianna began to describe the first part of it.

Each day of their birth month, October, they were going to be judged and graded. "Viewed," in Coventry terms. "Spied on," was Alex's take.

Either way, certain witches — their bio mom, Miranda; their guardian, Ileana; and the Exalted Elders of the island — would be able to see and hear them even when Cam and Alex were here in Marble Bay, Massachusetts, a thousand miles from Coventry.

Every choice the twins made — big or small, trivial or serious — would be monitored and evaluated.

Starting today, now, this very minute, Cam realized, her decisions, choices, and actions were already being viewed. She was supposed to be practicing her craft, trying to rack up points in applied magick. But practice only made perfect if what she did was done for the right reasons. Reasons that upheld the Coventry creed. "That all things might grow to their most bountiful goodness." That was supposed to be her guide, hers and Alex's, and the end result of all their decisions.

They were also, the buxom old witch had said, expected to know close to one hundred spells. Whether or not they used them was also their choice.

One hundred spells! Cam remembered how she'd begun to panic — until Miranda had tossed in the tidbit that all one hundred were variations on the basics: Truth, Travel, and Transformation.

Score! She and Alex had already done all of the above; in the past, they'd made use of the Big Three with excellent results.

Rhianna had overheard Cam's mental back-pat. That was when their Initiation Master had explained a crucial rule: No help.

Neither of the twins could get an assist from any

witch or warlock during their Initiation period. No way, no how, no matter how they tried to manipulate it.

Hearing the news, Alex had cut her eyes at Cam and sent a mind message: *Yo, that's messed up.*

"Deal with it," Rhianna had curtly advised. "Your Initiation begins on the first day of October —"

"But we've got school," Cam had interrupted.

Rhianna glanced at Miranda, who'd been standing between her daughters.

"Now is the time to listen and learn," their mother quickly urged them.

"In school and out, on the mainland and on Coventry," the winged witch clarified, to be sure they really understood, "your every act must include one or all of the following virtues: wisdom, intuition, trust, courage, and honesty. The more of these qualities you use in making your decisions, the more worthy you will be considered of being true witches."

"And the more stones you'll earn," Ileana had blurted.

Stones? Cam and Alex thought at once.

"Points," Miranda explained. "Each sacred stone is worth one point. And you must each earn one hundred during your Initiation month."

Wisdom. Intuition. Trust. Courage. Honesty. Twenty

points for each would do it, Cam had reckoned. Perfectionist that she was, she had itched to take notes. But Ileana caught the thought and, with a disapproving frown, shook her head no.

"That your choices must be steeped in sympathy and empathy goes without saying," Rhianna went on, "and that your decisions are made in a spirit of kindness, compassion, justice, and love. More than ever before, this is the time for you to come to the aid of your peers when they are in need. You are free to use all the magick at your command; in fact, you are encouraged to do so. Your memory of spells — of herbs, crystals, and incantations — will thus be honed."

A mind message from Ileana had warned that they'd better bone up on the entire contents of *The Little Book of Spells.*

"But it is your actions — when, where, and how you choose to use your gifts — that will most decide the outcome," Rhianna had added pointedly.

That was part one of their Initiation. Doing the Right Thing, it could have been called.

And then they were to be summoned to Coventry for part two, which Cam had instantly dubbed the Q&A.

There, at the Unity Dome with the entire population of the island looking on, any Elder could ask them any question about anything to do with their witchy heritage, powers, magick, and craft.

From alchemy, the fabled science of transformation and transmutation, to zircon, a false diamond not approved as a sacred stone, they were expected to know the history, ingredients, incantations, purposes, and powers of every spell, and when and how to use them.

After each answer, Rhianna had explained, the Elders would vote on how well they'd done. And whether they'd made the grade.

Exactly when would it take place? Cam had wondered silently.

"You will be called at the auspicious moment," Rhianna answered dismissively.

Just as Cam was about to ask what would happen if they blew a question or two, Rhianna delivered one last Initiation bulletin: There was a part three to the proceedings!

And it wasn't going to be anything as simple as an essay.

No number-two pencils to sharpen, no clock ticking, no teachers pacing the aisles. No chance to prepare, either, because, as it turned out, they would not even be *told* the topic of part three beforehand.

Ileana had tried to coax Rhianna into revealing

some small bit of info on the final phase, but the impatient older woman's wings ruffled menacingly and her piercing gaze had been enough to silence their guardian.

"We will not discuss that now," she announced firmly.

Whatever that part of their WATs was, they'd have to deal with it later. Not knowing was the worst, as far as Cam was concerned. She couldn't prep in any way. What if, for the first time in her life, she was faced with a test she couldn't ace?

"What happens if we . . . you know . . . fail?" she'd worked up the nerve to ask.

"You can take the test again," their mother had assured them. "Your uncle Fredo took it several times —"

"Yes, but as with your pitiful uncle, your powers will be diminished," Rhianna informed them. "Some of them will weaken after the first failure. And more will be lost after any later failures, until —"

"Until we have no magick left?" Cam asked weakly.

Reluctantly, their mother had said softly, "Yes."

"What happens if we pass?" Alex cut to the chase.

"Your powers will increase," Ileana said.

"You'll be able to help more and more people in need —" Miranda explained.

"No longer fledglings, you will be welcomed into our society as equals," Rhianna announced. "Our ancient and powerful community will nurture and protect you as long as you live."

"So that's it?" Alex had turned to Ileana. "We get spied on at home and do a Q&A here, and we're in?"

Before their guardian could respond, Lady Rhianna had slapped her hand down on a glass-front cabinet, causing it to shudder and tinkle, and causing the twins to swiftly face her again. "Apolla! Artemis!" Their birth names rolled like thunder in Rhianna's mouth. "As I told you, there will be one more test to face. It will tell us how well you handle . . . new situations. Situations that will present the most difficult yet valuable challenges you'll ever face."

"Why does it have to be a secret?" Cam had blurted, her nerves getting the best of her.

"Can't you at least tell us what form it will take?" Alex had backed Cam up.

Rhianna sighed mightily. Her cinnamon breath swept Cam's cheeks and ruffled Alex's seriously gelled hair.

"Lord Karsh, in his infinite but extremely bewildering wisdom, wished this on me," the wide, old, wise witch murmured. "That I should be your Initiation Master. That I should view and guide you during this momentous time. Why, is anyone's guess." She drew a deep breath. "As I said, your Initiation begins on the first day of your birth month and will culminate here on Coventry. I look forward to it.

You will be summoned at the proper time. For now, enjoy what's left of your summer."

In Marble Bay, Cam glanced again at the digital clock. *Today is the first day of the rest of your life.* The cheesy expression came to her — and it had never seemed so true.

CHAPTER THREE
THE IMPOSTER

Cam turned from the clock with a start. It seemed like only a few seconds since Alex had gone on her food-foraging expedition. Now here she was, banging open the door to their room — looking wild-eyed and furious.

"What?" Cam asked, annoyed at her sister's entrance.

"Leave that alone!" Alex commanded in a voice filled with venom. The vicious tone, in Cam's opinion, was totally over the top.

And so was the way Alex was glaring at her.

Cam was used to their constant bickering, but the way her sister's gray eyes were glinting spitefully at the book in Cam's hand made her skin crawl.

"Don't lose my place!" Alex snarled. "Put that book down! Now!"

Her twin could be unpredictable and hot-blooded, but she'd never before turned on Cam like a growling beast. Stunned, Cam slammed the little spell book shut. "What'd you get to eat, ground glass?" she responded defensively.

"None of your business!" Alex shocked her by shouting.

Something was way off. In addition to the twisted rage Alex had never expressed before, there seemed to be an icy draft streaming from her.

"Drop the book before you get hurt!" Alex the Angry ordered.

Without thinking twice, Cam hurled the fragile old book across the room at her sister.

The book stopped in midair, inches from Alex's face. It spun abruptly, did a U-ie, then sped with frightening velocity back in Cam's direction.

For a moment Cam stood paralyzed. Eyes wide with astonishment, she gaped at her twin. Then self-preservation kicked in and she ducked. The book slammed into the wall behind her, tearing a gash in her poster of hottie soccer star David Beckham.

* * *

Later that day, in the early evening, Alex was standing in the kitchen when Emily came in juggling three bags overflowing with groceries. She'd gone food shopping after work.

"Want to give me a hand?" the tottering woman asked.

"That'll be the day." The surly tone of Cam's voice as she entered the kitchen surprised both Alex and Emily. "She'd rather give you a foot — as in a kick."

Alex's response was quick and angry. "What are you doing here, on a sulking break?" she asked, relieving Emily of two bags of groceries and setting them on the kitchen island. Alex had barely spoken to Cam all day.

A peculiar odor had seeped into the room. What had Emily bought, Alex wondered, and why did it smell so strange yet familiar?

Flustered, but opting to play the peacemaker, Emily ignored their rancor. Hoping to change the subject, she asked with exaggerated innocence, "Have you girls thought about what you'd like to do for your birthday?"

"Alex has," Cam said in her nasty new incarnation. "She'd rather be dead than have a sweet sixteen party!"

Emily caught her breath. "Is that true?" she asked after a moment.

Alex barely heard the question. Her mouth was

open and her brow seriously creased as she studied her sister. Cam's metallic-gray eyes flashed back at her; behind them, her thoughts were purposefully scrambled, preventing Alex from knowing what was really on her mind. Before she could ask, Cam struck out again.

"What's wrong with your hyper-hearing? Didn't you get Mommy's question?"

Mommy? Alex thought. Cam had never called Emily "Mommy" before. Not ever.

And *hyper-hearing*? Her sister must've gone mental to mention one of Alex's special gifts in front of Emily, who knew nothing about their being witches. Was this Cam's idea of honesty — blowing their cover and letting Em in on way more than she could handle?

"Is that true, Alex? You . . . um, you don't like the idea?" Usually in command, confident, competent, and, face it, bossy, Emily was gnawing on her bottom lip like a hurt child and waiting apprehensively for Alex's answer.

Yes, they were supposed to be exercising rigorous honesty. But would sparing Emily's feelings really count as an out-and-out lie? No, Alex decided. It might even fall under kindness, compassion, justice, and love.

Alex felt a gust of cold air, like a draft, blowing from Cam's direction. Alex looked up to find her sister watching her, hands on her hips, lips curled in a snarl. "Don't even think about lying!" Cam said.

Emily seemed as startled as Alex by the bitterness in Cam's tone. "Do you feel the same way," she cautiously asked her daughter, "about . . . having a birthday party?"

"Let me think," Cam proposed sarcastically, placing an index finger on her cheek. "That would be . . . a yes."

"Camryn," Emily blurted, hurt.

"Get off my back," Cam growled.

David Barnes, Emily's husband and Cam's usually adoring adoptive dad, stalked into the kitchen. Clearly, he'd caught the tail end of the conversation and was rolling up his shirtsleeves as he came, as if unconsciously preparing for a fight. "How dare you talk to your mother that way?" he demanded.

"Did you say 'mother'?" Cam sneered. "Hello, I'm adopted."

Dave's face grew purple. He started to say something, then thought better of it. His bushy mustache flagged as his mouth clamped shut.

Alex glanced at Emily. The poor woman's eyes were swimming behind a veil of tears. Dave put his arm around her shoulder. "Em, excuse us for a minute," he whispered to his distraught wife. "I'd like to speak to them alone."

Emily nodded. She squared her shoulders bravely and lifted her chin and did not turn to look at either Cam or Alex as she marched out of the room.

"It's the truth!" Cam wailed as Emily left. "Alex said

terrible things about you and I just got so upset. I'd never have acted like that on my own. Oh, Mommy —"

Mommy? There it was again, Alex thought. What was Cam trying to pull?

"What's going on here?" Dave demanded. He knew the twins were witches. He had been told when the infant girl, who they'd named Camryn, had been given to him by the ancient warlock Karsh. He'd only learned of Alex's existence a year ago, when the same beloved old man left her — an angry, grieving teenager — literally on their doorstep.

"I'm sorry. I said I was sorry." Now it was Cam's turn to burst into tears.

Alex felt Dave's eyes on her. She shrugged. "Cam's been kind of upset lately," she offered. Dave was waiting for more. "About a boy," Alex continued cautiously. "Um, nothing big, just . . . a boy."

The moment Dave dismissed them, Cam dashed out of the room and up the stairs.

Something told Alex to leave her alone. To just drop the whole baffling episode.

Something was wrong. Cam was acting beyond weird. And the odor in the kitchen, the bittersweet stench Alex had thought was coming from the grocery bag — could it have been coming from Cam?

More perplexed than angry now, Alex decided to get out of the house, to cool off and give Cam a chance to chill, too.

As she stepped outside, Cam's brother, Dylan, was hiking up the driveway, droopy, wide pants dragging, skateboard under his arm. "Whassup?" he said. "You look like you just got jacked flipping off your back trucks."

Alex sighed and shook her head but could feel her mouth twitching into a smile. "English," she requested.

"Seriously, dude. You look really bummed."

"It's nothing," she insisted, hoping she was right.

CHAPTER FOUR
THE FIRST TEST

Except for another burst of angry accusations just before dinner, the twins avoided each other for the rest of the evening and barely spoke the next morning.

Cam stayed in bed pretending to be asleep until she heard Alex leave. Then she got up and took a quick shower. By the time she returned to the bedroom, her hair still dripping and a towel wrapped around her, Alex was back. And she was tossing their Coventry Island books into a big green garbage bag.

Cam was determined not to ask why, but she couldn't help wondering.

Which Alex quickly picked up on. Without pausing

or glancing at Cam, she announced, "You're on your own. I decided I'm not going to be initiated. So I won't need this stupid stuff."

There it was again — the hateful look, the malicious tone. . . .

Cam was stunned as, she supposed, her sister had meant for her to be. Determined to avoid another face-off, she turned away from Alex and toward the mirror over her dresser.

First she knew it instinctively, then she saw it in the mirror. Alex had stopped hurling books into the bag and was staring at her — with a terrible, calculating glare. A look so malevolent it was hard to believe it was Alex.

Chills ripped through Cam's spine. She shuddered in a sudden cold current that seemed to be flowing from her sister.

But couldn't be.

More likely, she decided, the problem was her wet hair. Shivering, she hurried back into the bathroom to dry it. As she turned off the blow-dryer, the bedroom door slammed. Her sister had stalked out again, leaving the bag of books on the floor between their beds.

Dylan was wolfing down a forbidden Pop-Tart when Alex entered the kitchen. "Don't tell Mom, okay?" he asked, spraying crumbs in his hurry to make her his ally. "She thinks they rot your brain. I stashed a couple behind the oatmeal. Want one?"

"Believe me, I don't need any sugar this morning," Alex said. "My adrenaline is doing push-ups thanks to your sister."

"Cam? What'd she do?"

"Tried to play psycho games with me! She was totally weird yesterday. And then, just before supper, she went ballistic. Said I threw a book at her. Which I did not!" Alex grabbed a container of orange juice from the fridge. "I don't know what's going on, but she better stay out of my way today."

"Ballistic? You sure it was Cam?" Dylan was equally amused and surprised. "Dude, she must be having some kind of meltdown. Losing control is so not her M.O."

"I'm sure," Alex confirmed.

But all of a sudden, she wasn't.

Dylan caught her hesitation, her questioning look. "What?" he asked.

Alex shrugged. The moment of doubt passed. "Nothing," she said. "Maybe I'm losing it, too."

Cam and Alex left the house at different times, by different doors just to be sure. When they passed each other in the hall at school, they looked the other way. Cam made a point of laughing loudly with her best bud Beth when Alex walked by. When she saw Cam coming, Alex stuck her head into her locker so quickly that she practically impaled herself on a hook.

At least they didn't have to try to avoid each other at lunch. While Cam held court at the popular table with her crew, the Six Pack, Alex was meeting Cade at the soccer field to munch lunch and catch up.

Cade Richman. Just thinking of him made her smile in spite of herself and her sister's sudden strangeness.

Cade was the first guy who really got her. And got *to* her. The dark-haired, blue-eyed boy pierced right through her tough exterior.

She'd gotten an e-mail from him that morning suggesting face-time, and she'd been all over it. Between homework and his after-school internship at a law firm, they hadn't seen a whole lot of each other lately.

Cade had volunteered to bring sandwiches. Alex stopped by the cafeteria to pick up a supersized brownie and a couple of sodas.

Sure enough, Cam was with her squad, totally into whatever her pal Bree was gushing about. Without wanting to, Alex was suddenly tuned in to the chat.

Bree was dissing Nadine Somerfeld, the new girl at

school, who was sitting alone two tables away. According to the pint-sized fashionista, Nadine's outfit was "thrift-shop generic or budget mall-wear at best."

To her credit, Cam wasn't having any. She rounded irritably on Bree and told her to chill. Her sister must have sensed Alex's presence nearby because she turned just then and, as her eyes met Alex's, the irritability drained away and Cam's look became one of sadness and longing.

For me? Alex wondered, surprised by the pull that eye contact with her twin was having on her.

Mindlessly, Alex toyed with her moon amulet. The hammered-gold charm matched the sun necklace Cam always wore. Together the two pieces, moon and sun, formed a perfect circle. Occasionally, they seemed to have wills of their own — heating up and reaching toward each other. Like now, Alex realized.

What's happening to us? she heard her twin ask telepathically.

I don't know, Alex admitted, despite not wanting to answer, stubbornly wanting to hang on to their griev-ances.

She glanced at the lunchroom clock and decided that she ought to get going. Cade would be waiting.

Something weird's going on, Als, she heard her sister thinking.

Tell me about it, Alex sent back sarcastically. She picked up the brownie, got two sodas from the machine, and left the cafeteria without looking back at Cam.

Cade was late, which wasn't like him. Alex took another sip of soda and scoped out the grounds again.

From her vantage point at the top of the bleachers, she could see pretty much all there was to see: the side of the school building, all bricks and ivy; the sports center, looking slapped on and out of place like a grounded gleaming spaceship; the track and playing fields. The field in front of her, where a couple of kids were kicking a ball around, was Cam's turf — the arena of her sister's soccer stardom.

And now strolling across it was Cade.

With Cam!

They were laughing. Yukking it up. So entertained by each other that they were totally oblivious of Alex — and the shock of searing anger reddening her face.

How had her newly bizarre sister split the lunch-room so fast? When and where had Cam latched on to Cade? And why was her arm, right this minute, sliding through Cade's and clamping it with her Perfectly-Pink-tipped grip?

Cam looked up. Her lips twisted into an ugly smirk as she caught sight of Alex's expression.

What do you think you're doing? Alex sent a terse telepathic shout-out.

Excuse me? Cam blinked; her face shifted slyly from evil to innocent. *I looked the boy-toy over but, whoops, I guess I missed your Property-Of stamp.*

Seething, Alex glanced at Cade. He was looking up at her, slack-jawed, his usually lively baby blues staring blankly.

You cast a spell on him! she accused her sister.

Cam laughed. *You said we had to practice for our Initiation, didn't you?*

Alex felt it again: the same cold breeze that had set her shivering in the kitchen yesterday. And, as Cam drew nearer, the same stinging scent, a strange earthy smell that burned her nostrils and made her eyes water.

Jimsonweed and nettles! Alex thought, surprised and pleased at her herbal recall.

Not Cade's scent. Not Cam's, either.

Instinctively, Alex seized her moon charm. She grasped it so tightly that it bit into her palm. Heedless of the pain, she glared at her sister, half expecting, half daring Cam to reach for her sun charm.

The two amulets had always been used in tandem, to magnify their magick. Now Alex feared Cam might use hers to set off a battle of wills.

But her twin didn't reach for her gold charm. Her

twin, Alex suddenly realized, wasn't wearing the powerful necklace at all. She must have taken it off when she met up with Cade.

Taken aback but relieved, Alex ordered: "Undo it, Cam! Undo the spell. Right now!"

As if the sound of her voice had roused him, Cade blinked. The film that had dulled his eyes lifted. "Hey," he said, looking at Alex with a radiant smile, "there you are. I'm . . ." He turned his head, twisted his neck as if the muscles were tight. "I don't know what happened. I . . . I just started feeling . . . strange. Like instant flu or something —"

"Poor baby," Cam said tenderly to Cade. "That's why I walked you here. You were standing in front of your locker looking totally sick and desperately in need of TLC. Well —" she crooned, grinning like a demented smiley face, "have a nice day."

"We've got to talk," Alex said after school that day, crashing into their room and winging her backpack onto her overburdened bed.

"You said it!" Cam spun around in her computer chair to glare at her sister.

"What's going on?!" they demanded at the same time.

"Excuse me?" Cam said indignantly.

"Right back atcha!" Alex growled.

"Okay. Time-out." Cam made a T sign with her hands. "Why does Emily think I don't want a sweet sixteen party?"

"Duh, let me think." Alex laid a finger along her cheek exactly as Cam had done during their kitchen confrontation. "Because you told her so?"

"No way!" Cam was exasperated.

"Right after you told her I'd rather be dead than go to a sweet sixteen party."

"Put on your pj's, Alex — you must be dreaming!"

"And I suppose I dreamed up your flirting with Cade today?"

"Like I dreamed up your telling Beth I thought she needed to get her hair cut by a person instead of a hay mower? I couldn't believe you came to soccer practice this afternoon and said that right in front of me! Everyone thought you'd gone mental!"

"Soccer practice? I don't know what you're trying to pull," Alex snapped back. "I didn't go near your Six Pack of snotty sycophants —"

"Sycophants? What'd you interrupt your Coventry reading for, a quick dip in the dictionary? Oops, I forgot. You're not getting initiated —"

"Oh, really? Who gave you that flash?"

They were breathing hard, glaring at each other,

their hands balled into fists, mouths moving faster than their brains.

A familiar fragrance wafted off Cam — a clean, crisp scent of chamomile, rosemary, and sweet violets, the scent Alex recognized as her sister's. Which reinforced the certainty that the stinging spicy odor that had hit her on the bleachers had not been Cam's. Nor had it been Cade's warm, fresh scent.

Alex felt the hot rage draining from her. "Cam, don't you feel it? Something's up," she blurted.

"Something's off," Cam agreed. Her hands uncurled, her hunched fight-or-flight shoulders dropped as she faced . . . her sister. Her identical twin. Her Alex. "I've been trying to tell you that."

Alex's metallic-gray eyes never left Cam's. "The only thing radically new in our lives is that our Initiation's started. Maybe whatever's going on is part of that. I mean, do you think this is some kind of test?"

"Not a bad idea." The thought, spoken aloud in a strong, ringing voice, was Lady Rhianna's. The Coventry Elder was staring into a large, jagged crystal. In the faceted stone she, and the impulsive young witch breathing down her neck, had seen the twins facing off at each other.

Rhianna sneezed — then frowned accusingly at Boris,

the marmalade cat in Ileana's arms. "Someone is playing a trick on Camryn and Alexandra," she managed to say before sneezing again.

"It's unfair, unjust!" Ileana cried with such passion that Boris leaped off her, screeching and hissing, his orange hackles raised. "Someone is setting them against each other. Forcing them to act out of anger," she fumed.

Rhianna raised her eyebrows. "A topic you know a bit about," she chided.

But the beautiful young witch didn't take the bait. "We've got to warn them. This is not a rehearsal — they're being viewed right now!"

"So they are," the Elder continued, relieved that the cat, to which she was allergic, had scampered away. "And even though we didn't plan this, I say we don't interfere. It will be a perfect — if unexpected — test of intuition for them to flush out and deal with this wild card they've been dealt."

"It's a bad idea," the twin's guardian asserted hotly. "A very bad idea! Someone is cheating! Someone with a stake in ruining my charges' Initiation!"

"My charges! So it's all about Ileana." Rhianna pulled a cloth purposefully over the crystal. She was scowling at Ileana but couldn't help remembering that the girl, the beautiful and impetuous child, had been Karsh Antayus's adored fledgling.

As it always did when she thought of her old, now-departed friend, Rhianna's heart softened. "Lady Ileana," she began. Then her eyes twinkled as she recalled what Karsh had confided to her, that the brazen young witch had rejected the title. No lady was their Ileana.

Rhianna cleared her throat but could not hide her smile. "I understand you prefer to be called goddess." She tried to sound serious.

Ileana's jaw dropped. She got as far as "But how —?" Then realizing that it must have been Karsh who'd told Rhianna, she burst into tears.

Which nearly brought tears to Rhianna's eyes as well. "Yes, yes," the wise old witch said, honking into her handkerchief. "We all miss him, Ileana. And we all share Lord Karsh's certainty that Aron's daughters are most magnificent fledglings and destined for leadership —"

"If that black-bearded, two-faced, cold-blooded brute doesn't find a way to stop them," Ileana shot back.

Rhianna raised her brows again. "I assume you're speaking of your father?"

"Who else stands to gain if Apolla and Artemis fail their Initiation? Of course it's Thantos who's behind this."

"Does this mean you believe they *can* fail?" Rhianna asked pointedly. "You, their guardian and champion? Surely you know them as well as anyone."

Ileana saw the tricky old witch's point. And had to

consider it. Did she think that Thantos, her merciless father and the twins' uncle, could best them? Well, he'd certainly put in a good effort.

Ileana remembered the first day of the infants' lives, when she and Karsh had hidden in the snowy woods with the babies, listening to the approaching clatter of Thantos and his bloodthirsty horde. He had not found them then. She recalled Karsh's tale of how the twins had discovered each other, when once again, they'd escaped their uncle's trap. And later, in Marble Bay when her treacherous father had tried to lure the twins to him. And again and again.

Thantos had known all along that they, not he, had been chosen to lead their family. They and only they, two bright, still vulnerable young witches, fledglings, stood in the way of his grasping what he believed, *wanted* to believe, belonged to him — the wealth and power of the DuBaer dynasty.

He also knew, as did everyone on the island, that once the twins were initiated, their destiny — and his — would be sealed.

"Maybe he's just been unlucky so far," she told Rhianna, knowing how unlikely that sounded.

As they always did when her feathers were ruffled, the Exalted Elder's wings suddenly unfurled. The *whoosh*

of wind, a sound like the slap of sails filling in a squall, made Ileana jump back.

"First of all," Rhianna sternly lectured, "we do not believe in luck! We create our own good fate through right choices and actions."

It was all Ileana could do not to roll her eyes at the old saying.

"Yes, it was your grandfather Nathaniel's wish, and your guardian Karsh's mission, to place the girls where they might do the most good — at the helm of your extremely powerful and, may I say, increasingly troublesome family. They have but to pass their Initiation — which you and their mother assured me they will do with flying colors — to take their rightful place in our community."

"Of course they'll pass," Ileana blurted. "But why should they be subjected to different and more difficult tests than other fledglings?"

"Because I say so," Rhianna declared, leading Ileana to the door. "And I, not you, Ileana DuBaer, am their Initiation Master — exactly as Lord Karsh intended for me to be."

CHAPTER FIVE
THE THIRD TWIN

"Do you think we were triplets?" Cam asked skeptically.

Alex shook her head. "No way. Everyone on Coventry, including our mother," she pointed out, "says we were twins. No mention of a third party."

Someone was playing them. Someone witchy. They'd been talking about it all weekend, trying to figure it out. Now, standing in front of Cam's school locker Monday afternoon, the debate continued.

"Could it be a clone then?" Cam said. They'd gotten that far in their thinking. "Someone going around trying to make me believe she's you — and then impersonating me when you and I are not in the same room. But how?"

"And who? And why?" Alex added. "And what am I supposed to have done today?"

The twins had called a tentative truce Sunday night so they could check out some of the reading material they'd rescued from the green garbage bag — which Alex had insisted she'd never seen before. She also, she'd claimed, had no intention of quitting, of ducking out on their Initiation, no matter what Cam had hallucinated.

"You insulted Bree at lunch," Cam reported. "She was bragging about how valuable her advice was to her father and how he'd hired this studly star for his new movie just 'cause Bree told him to."

"And I ruined her life how?" Alex waited for the explanation.

"You said, 'Get over yourself, Pinocchio — your surgically improved nose is growing. Your dad couldn't care less what you think.'"

"Ugh, that's ugly," Alex agreed. "And 'you' did your usual diss on my outfit." She struck a pose, showing off the flannel shirt covering her sleeveless black tee, scruffy jeans, and scuffed Doc Marten boots. "You called me a goth cow, which I thought was way much and so out of date."

"Okay, let's review," Cam proposed, lowering her voice as a crew of noisy juniors swept past. "We can't be in two places at once —"

"Unless," Alex mused, "we stumbled into some kind of spell. You know, like, said the wrong thing without realizing it or handled a weird combo of crystals and herbs —"

"We checked the books," Cam reminded her. "There wasn't one spell in them that could have given us personality transplants."

Cam shook her head. "I mean, I know for absolute certain that I never put a spell on Cade. Please. That is so ridiculous. I mean, you saw me in the lunchroom, right? When would I have had time to get all next to him and then put him in a trance? Wasn't me," she asserted, pulling her art portfolio out of her locker. In about fifteen minutes, they *would* be in two places at once — they'd be in two different classrooms.

"Yes, and . . . ?" Alex prompted, having picked up on Cam's thought.

"The thing, the clone, whatever it is, only attacks us when we're separated," Cam explained. "Which we will be again the minute you're in chem lab and I'm in Mrs. Wagner's art class . . . unless —" Her striking gray eyes lit with sudden inspiration. "Unless we hang together —"

"Right." Alex made a face. "I'll just cut lab and show up unexpectedly for art with you. And my excuse will be?"

"No, no. We can't stay together physically. But what if —" Cam was on it — "we keep in touch telepathically, check in every couple of minutes?" Even though she wasn't a fabulous mind reader, Cam had been able to tune in to her sister's thoughts for a while now.

"Sounds like a plan," Alex said, "especially since the bell's about to ring."

A few minutes later, standing at one of the sinks in the chemistry lab, Alex heard Cam ask, *Having a good time, Madame Curie?*

Excellent, Alex sent back. *Wearing rubber gloves and safety goggles really does it for me. How 'bout you?*

There was no answer.

Cam, Alex tried again. *You okay? . . . Hello, can you hear me? . . . Cam, what's up? . . . Come on, you're freaking me.*

"Hello, I'm right here," an impatient voice said. Alex looked up to see her sister glaring at her across the lab table. The moment she caught Alex's eye, her expression changed to one of terrible pity.

"What are you doing here? How'd you get out of art?" Alex asked, looking around for Mr. Calio, the chem teacher. He was working with a couple of kids at the other end of the room.

"Oh, Alex, I'm so sorry —" Cam bit her lip, looked away, then turned bravely back to her sister. "It's awful. But you've got to know. I just went to my locker to get my portfolio —"

"Another portfolio?" Alex asked. "What happened to the one you had before?"

Cam blinked at her. "It doesn't matter. There was a note in my locker. From Cade. I don't know how to tell you this —"

Alex's heart flopped, fell like a busted elevator plummeting down a chute. "What?" she said.

"It's over. He wants to break up with you, but he's afraid that you'll totally tank. He's really a nice guy, Als. He's just not all that wild about you anymore."

It wasn't Cam.

Just five minutes ago at her locker, Cam had been wearing her sun necklace. This . . . this creature . . . wasn't. And her gray eyes were cold, colder than Cam's had ever been. And again there was the scent of nettles and jimsonweed. A fragrance Alex remembered, she was sure now, from her last trip to Coventry.

She wasn't that experienced with scrambling her thoughts, but she closed her eyes and pictured an iron door and willed it to slam shut over her brain.

Score one for intuition! The scheme must've worked. The Cam clone before her, pretending concern but really gloating, seemed to think that Alex had bought her story.

"Dude, I can't believe it," Alex said, glad that the

odor of the girl, or whatever it was, had set her eyes stinging again. A few tears would go a long way toward convincing the pretender of Alex's misery — which had obviously been sham Cam's goal.

"Are you mad at me for telling you?" the phony asked, not able to hide the hope in her voice. "I mean, just 'cause Cade chose to confide in me. . . ."

Whatever this Cam-copying creep was after, Alex was over it. She wanted to get rid of the counterfeit and check in with her real twin. Who knew what miserable hoax the two-faced twerp might've pulled on Cam?

But Alex played along. "Yeah. I'm mad at you, okay? I'm so mad that I'm —"

"Not going to Coventry, right?" The clone pulled a dejected face, but her eyes were alive with expectation. "You don't even want to be initiated, do you?"

Bingo! That took care of *why.* Someone didn't want Alex taking her witch vows. All she and Cam had to figure out now was *who* and *how.*

"Yo, dude, you have so got my number," Alex told the girl who would be Cam. "I wouldn't set foot on Coventry now if . . . if . . . if some enchanted nut ball begged me to!"

Her make-believe "twin" looked confused.

"No Initiation, no way!" Alex insisted. "Now *hasta la vista,* babe, before Mr. Calio catches you here."

45

*   *   *

"Well, that really worked," Cam groused when they met on the front steps of the school. "I heard you for a minute, then there was nothing but static. I almost ran out of class to find out what happened."

"But you didn't because?"

"You know," she accused. "You sent that snotty note saying I was a lousy mind reader and you didn't need my help."

"Cami, that wasn't me. I didn't send any note."

"Excuse me. I think I know your handwriting," Cam insisted. But after a beat, she added in a whisper, "It was her, wasn't it?"

Alex nodded. "Our new 'twin.' The deal is she's here to turn us against each other," she continued, heading down the walk to the street, "and, more important, to keep us — or maybe just me — from going through with our Initiation. I'm sure of it. Now who would want to keep us from going back to Coventry?"

Cam didn't have to think about it. "First guess? Uncle T. Although I can't imagine him turning himself into one of us. He's way too arrogant —"

"But he wouldn't think twice about sending someone else to do his dirty work. It's practically become a habit with him," Alex pointed out. "Bottom line, the ringer doesn't want one or both of us to show for our Initiation."

"You know, Als," Cam said hesitantly, "sometimes I'm not sure I want to go through with it, anyway. . . . I mean, what's really in it for us?"

Alex stared hard at her sister — if it *was* her sister, she thought.

"Hello, it's me," Cam shot back, waving her hands in front of Alex's face. "Cam I am, Cam I am — I do not like always being in a jam!"

"Cute." Alex was convinced. Their unknown nemesis didn't have much of a sense of humor. They'd passed PITS, their favorite pizza hangout, and the CD superstore Music & More, and were walking up the hill toward home. "Well," she began, responding to Cam's query, "first of all, they say our magick'll get much stronger —"

"Do we need it to be?" Cam asked.

Abruptly she flashed back to how she'd saved her best friend Beth's life. And halted a trio of preteen troublemakers playing with firecrackers from blowing their hands off. And, yes, it was clear that the stronger her powers were, the easier it would be to play Wonder Cam, showing up for kids who needed help.

"But you said before, maybe this . . . thing . . . wants to stop just you — or me. Why would that —" Before she finished the question, Cam knew the answer: She hadn't rescued the pyromaniac brat pack alone last summer. She, in person, and Alex from a distance together had conjured up the spell that saved the kids. And together they'd once stopped a calamity at a Ferris wheel. The common adverb? *Together.*

Cam remembered how exciting it had been, the thrilling jolt, the raw adrenaline rush of focusing all her energy and skill on helping someone in trouble. How much more could she do, she and Alex, when their knowledge of the craft and the amazing powers they were born with got kicked up a notch?

She might not need her powers to be enhanced, but did she want them to be? Enough to study this hard and face —

"Every witch and warlock on the island judging us?" her sister anticipated the question.

Cam smiled and shrugged. "I think I can handle it. How 'bout you?"

"I'm on," Alex agreed as they walked along the tree-lined street to their house. Fallen leaves crunched under-foot, but the sugar maple, against which Dylan's bike was leaning, was still aflame.

Cam stopped at the front door as another memory surfaced for her. This one wasn't about anyone else — except Alex. She remembered how frightening and lonely it had been to feel like a freak. To have no one to talk to about the strange things she seemed capable of. The Mutant of Marble Bay, she'd sometimes thought of herself.

"Yo, and I was the Crow Creek Crazy." Alex invaded her sister's mind again. "What's your point?"

"That we're family, not weird and alone," Cam said.

"Gotcha. We're weird and together."

"Totally." Cam laughed and then speculated, "And if we were separated again, I bet we'd go right back to feeling alone and out of place everywhere."

"Except on Coventry," Alex reminded her twin — and herself. "Which, by the way, is where our clone comes from," she added. "Today, in lab, I remembered the smell — jimsonweed and nettles. I remember it from there — from Crailmore, I think."

"Crailmore?" Her hand reaching for the brass doorknob, Cam stopped, interested. "Okay, who do we know who hangs out at the ancestral fortress besides Thantos and our mom?"

"The Furies," Alex answered, naming the trio of treacherous witches they'd tangled with before. "Sersee, Michaelina, and Epie, but last time we saw them they were not fans of Uncle T. And Shane, of course — who changes his story every five minutes about whose side he's on."

"He is a sleaze, sad but true," Cam lamented. She

opened the door. "Then there are Uncle T's servants: the guy with the ponytail who was copying Karsh's journal for him, and his trusty fledgling Amaryllis —"

Alex cut through the speculation. "Look, the fact that our demon look-alike has never shown up when we're together gives us a way to flush the monster out. But where and when?"

"How 'bout our room? Tonight?" Sick and tired of being toyed with, Cam was suddenly psyched.

"Kind of ambitious." Alex followed her into the house.

"No, no. Come on. We can do it," Cam assured her sister.

"Yo, Cam-petition, check your cheerleading at the door," Alex advised. "This is not a game of soccer we're talking about —"

"Exactly!" Cam responded, her gray eyes already glimmering with gung-ho zeal. "It's an emergency! I don't know about you, but I can't deal with deception, keep up with schoolwork, and study for Initiation all at the same time —"

"Is that you?" Emily called from the kitchen. She was rarely home this early. "Don't come in," she ordered, sounding both alarmed and elated. "I'll be right out."

Alex and Cam looked at each other. "We've got to let

her know we know about the sweet sixteen," Cam whispered.

Alex vetoed the suggestion with a shake of her head. "We're going upstairs," she called to Emily. "Catch ya later."

Cam scampered up the stairs behind her twin. "Well, something's gotta go!" she hissed, back on track. "I vote that it's our third 'twin.'"

CHAPTER SIX
A SIMPLE PLAN

Alex gave in. Much as she hated to admit it, Cam's enthusiasm was contagious as the flu.

The plan they came up with was simple. They'd pull one of their traditional clashes. Then, as if disgusted, one of them would stomp out of their room, loudly slamming the door. The other would stay alone as bait. "Like a big, juicy, stinky hunk of cheese waiting for a rat," was how Alex delicately put it.

"And that would be me," Cam said, shaking her head at her sister's imagery.

"Who said?" Alex wanted to know.

"Who usually stomps out of our room, loudly slamming the door?" Cam asked.

"Point taken. I'll vanish," Alex agreed.

Alex would then slip through Dylan's room into the bathroom that linked his space with theirs. She would lie low there and listen for the clone to show up pretending to be her. Cam would be the bait, Alex the trap. At a signal from Cam, she'd pounce.

Then both of them would be in the room together. With their third "twin."

The creature couldn't pretend to be Alex with the real Alex standing right there.

The intruder would have to come clean.

Simple.

But not easy.

For starters, Alex and Cam would have to keep in touch telepathically — piece of cake — but this time they'd have to do it without allowing the witchy stranger to pick up their thoughts. It was obvious he or she had done just that while the girls tried to communicate in school.

"Did you ever try to *send* a vision?" Alex asked hopefully. With her amazing eyesight, Cam was a whiz at seeing things nobody else could see. Things that were too far away, both in distance and time. Tuning in to the future was just one of her specialties. "You know, like you could think of an image and then concentrate really hard on sending it to me."

Cam seemed puzzled. "Like scanning and e-mailing a photo?"

"Sorta. Think it, then forward it." Alex clarified.

Cam wasn't exactly experienced with calling up visions on demand. They usually took her by surprise, their arrival signaled by dizziness and a splitting headache. But she guessed it was worth a try. Closing her eyes tightly, she tried to see into the dark.

There was nothing but the usual blackness broken by flashes and dots of meaningless light. She opened her eyes and shook her head.

Alex sighed, discouraged. A second later, she snapped her fingers and said, "Got it!"

Cam looked skeptical.

"No, really," Alex assured her. "I did it today. The copycat was pretending to be you in chem lab and I muted my thoughts by imagining an iron door clanging shut on them. It'd be a cinch for you to do — picturing stuff is your thing."

"Scrambling our thoughts is not the hard part," Cam pointed out. "It's how to keep them from being intercepted by the clone."

"I know, I know. But wait. Just listen." Alex was flying by the seat of her pants, but flying nonetheless. "We can imagine the iron door, okay? But with a peephole in it! You know, the kind that you can open and close. Then, when we want to talk to each other, we imagine opening the little flap and kind of sneak our thoughts through."

Cam rolled her eyes.

"Dude, it's the best we've come up with so far. Try it. Close your eyes and picture a big, bad, two-ton iron door. Only with a little eye-level opening in it. Oh, yeah, and just to add that mojo edge, let's hold on to our charms."

Closing her eyes, Cam grasped her amulet and did as she was told.

"Okay, now think something." Alex ordered. "Let's see if I can 'hear' it."

Cam's face pruned with concentration, then she laughed.

"What?!" Alex demanded. "Whatever you find so amusing, I don't get it. So the door thing actually works, right?" Cam nodded, and Alex said, "Now the hard part. Try the peephole."

In her mind's eye, Cam imagined herself pushing the flap aside and peering through the thick door. To her astonishment, what she saw on the other side of the peephole was Alex!

Is it working? she heard her sister ask.

If you can hear this, it is, Cam thought. Grinning,

she eyed Alex's newly dyed, gelled-back, pitch-black locks gleefully and sent again the message her sister had missed before.

"I did not use shoe polish on my hair!" Alex exploded, psyched despite herself. "And I do not look like a helmet head!"

Cam's eyes flew open. "I think it might work!" she said.

So when replica girl shows up," Alex proposed, "you can call me through the peephole. I'll rush in. Then we can . . . what?" she wondered aloud. "Do the Transformer!" she announced a second later, congratulating herself on the idea. "Excellent. We can do the Transformation spell in reverse, change the clone back into whoever or whatever she really is!"

"Alex," Cam began, "I hate to rain on your brainstorm —"

"No, no. This'll be great," her sister informed her, busily rummaging through their Coventry books in search of, Cam assumed, *The Morphing and Transformation Handbook.* "Okay," Alex said, having found the weighty volume and riffled through its pages. "Here it is. This'll be the bomb."

"Hello! The Transformer doesn't work on human beings. It's like a really basic morph," Cam reminded her sister, remembering that they had used the spell once before — to change a frog Sersee had turned into a stick of wood back to its native form. "Only trackers can *transmutate* people. We can only renovate 'less evolved' things."

Alex recognized the procedure in the book. Cam was right. "What's 'less evolved' than the loser who's stalking us?" Alex challenged, undaunted. "Come on, it'll be a breeze. We already know the incantation. Let's try it."

Cam saw the mad glint in her sister's exceptional gray eyes.

She wasn't feeling too centered herself. Stress and lack of sleep had taken their toll. She was starting to feel nearly giddy.

"Try it on what?" Cam gave in. Checking out the room for something harmless, she spotted a pencil. "How about this?"

"Too easy," Alex decreed. "Let's push the envelope. Try it on something . . . um, slightly more evolved," she suggested, grinning.

"And that would be?" Cam tossed the pencil back onto her desk.

"You," her sister decided.

"Not even!" Cam spun to face her twin.

"I won't mess you up. I'll just, like, change your hair color or something easy like that. If it works, game over; the good guys win. If not, what have we got to lose?" Alex explained. "You're the one who said it doesn't work on human beings, remember? Yo, just stand still a second."

"Not a shot," Cam declared. "In the lab rat runoffs, I vote for you. You stand still and I'll cast the spell. How'd you like to trade in your grunge wear for a ruffles-and-chiffon frilly-blond, princess look?"

"About as much as you'd like spiky green streaks," Alex retorted, wild-eyed and wired. "Let's do it on each other!"

Bubbling suddenly with punch-drunk laughter, they ran to opposite ends of the room, eyed each other, sent the message *Go!*, and recited the Transformation incantation.

Nothing happened.

For a moment.

Then Alex began to get hot and incredibly itchy. She scratched her arms and then her waist and watched with her mouth open as Cam exploded in ugly red welts.

Catching a glimpse of her hives in the mirror, Cam shrieked at the top of her lungs, "Now are you satisfied?!"

"Okay, we messed up," Alex admitted, scratching behind her ear. "We'll try something else."

They never lost sight of each other at dinner. And the sight was better than they'd thought it would be.

Reversing the Transformer had proved fairly easy. Cam's hives had subsided, leaving her looking minorly bumpy, flushed but functional. Alex had a few itchy patches remaining.

The only one to comment on the aftermath of the spell was Dylan. "Dudes, 'sup with the rashes?" he asked, midway through the meat loaf.

Cam blurted the first thing that came to mind. "Leaf fight," she announced.

Bewildered, everyone stared at her, waiting.

"We were horsing around, throwing leaves at each other. Must've been poison ivy in the mix," Alex bailed her out. "Pass the veggies. Please."

Dylan left the table early. He had an English paper due in the morning. Emily was in an unusually cheerful mood. "Hypothetically," she said as Cam and Alex cleared their plates, "if, say, Beth or Bree were having a birthday party, where do you think the best place to hold it would be?"

Cam glanced at Alex. *Don't do it,* Alex warned her. *Don't tell her you already know.*

Like just forget about honesty, right? Cam shot back. *Anyway, I was just going to say, "Well, if it was my party . . ."*

"What's wrong with having it at home?" Dave dove in.

Oh, for goodness' sake, who asked you? The agitated thought Alex picked up was Emily's.

"Of course, what do I know?" Dave allowed, drawing back as if he, too, had read his wife's mind. He didn't have to. Emily's eyes flashed at him.

"You've probably got homework to do," he said to the twins. "Why don't you go on upstairs now. We can do the dishes."

"On the birthday bash front," Cam burst out, "I'd opt for a more exotic locale."

Alex grabbed her arm. "It's too bad it's not our party," she said, dragging her sister out of the kitchen. "Leaf fight?!" she asked as soon as they were in the hall.

"It was the best I could do," Cam fired back, breaking free of Alex's grasp. "Which was way better than stupefied silence followed by the witty poison ivy add-on."

They didn't have to fake a fight. Cam was steaming when they got to their room.

"By the way, what I say or do about *my* birthday party is none of your business," she growled. "You don't care what kind of bender they throw. You're not even gonna show, right?"

"It's the principle of the thing," Alex asserted. "Can't you see how psyched Emily is about this? You want to deflate her totally? Why don't you just throw a spell on her?

You could do what you did to Sersee. Only instead of blowing her up, you could puncture Emily's balloon and leave her a shriveled mess."

"Ooh, I'm so bad," Cam said sarcastically, but her sister's reference to the dirty trick she'd played on the Coventry witch had hit its mark.

A minute's "fun" had cost Cam hours of regret. She'd been talked into behaving vengefully, cruelly. She'd used, or rather, abused her gifts to cause someone else pain.

An' it harm none, had been their father Aron's motto. *That all things may grow to their most bountiful goodness,* was the Coventry creed. In that one act of reckless revenge, she'd trashed both beliefs.

She and Shane had cast the spell on Sersee — who undoubtedly deserved it. And they'd watched with glee as the vain witch swelled to revolting proportions. The worst moment? When Amaryllis had entered with a wheelbarrow to cart out the bloated, humiliated girl.

It was almost fitting, Cam thought now, that Amaryllis, one of Thantos's sordid servants, had later joined forces with Sersee to try to destroy Cam and Alex.

Amaryllis. Cam shuddered, remembering how the girl had kept watching her, studying her every move and gesture.

Amaryllis? Alex had picked up on the name. She

cocked her head and tried to coax out a thought that lurked at the back of her brain. It refused to budge, leaving her with only a vague uneasiness.

"Enough!" she called a halt to Cam's reminiscences. "Climb off the pity pot, Cam-ille, and grab your sun charm."

It was time to set the copycat trap. Alex envisioned the steel door and, holding on to her moon charm, sent a message through the peephole to Cam. *Let's get it on. Time to smoke out the lone clone.*

It's not going to be all that hard to act like I can't stand you, Cam sniped silently.

Just do the door, her twin ordered telepathically.

Cam took a deep breath, shut her eyes, and pictured an iron barrier protecting her thoughts. Dutifully, she drilled the peephole through it. *Can you read me now?* she sent.

Like a trashy novel, Alex hurled back. *How 'bout you? Obnoxiously loud and clear! Okay, let's go audio.*

Alex was ready. "You know, you're a spoiled brat," she loudly declared for whoever might be listening.

"You mean someone used to the good life," Cam replied in her most believably snotty voice, "as opposed to trailer trash from Montana? Oops. I didn't mean 'trailer' — no, I forgot, it's called a 'modular dwelling,' isn't it?"

"Baap!" Alex imitated a buzzer going off. "Big-time

compassion lapse. That's about thirty points shaved off your Initiation total. Don't play me, Cam, I'm feeling extremely hair-trigger."

"What do you care how many points I win or lose, you're not even going to be initiated! As for hair-trigger?" Cam sneered, "you should've pulled the trigger on that 'do —"

"Don't go there," Alex warned.

"Speaking of go, why don't you?" her sister suggested. "Just 'cause you're flaking doesn't mean *I'm* not going to be initiated —"

"And make mainland honor role, too?" Alex mocked in her most viciously superior tone.

"Totally. Which means I've got tons of studying to do. So buh-bye, little Miss Fledgling Forever. Don't you have elsewhere to be?"

"Anywhere you're not!" Alex shot back, clomping loudly to the door. With her hand on the knob, she paused to mouth, "Good luck" to her sister, then left, slamming the door behind her.

CHAPTER SEVEN
THE UNDOING

How totally out of it were they? Alex wondered the minute she burst into Dylan's room and found him sitting at his computer.

They hadn't figured on his being there! Hadn't thought twice about it when the bro excused himself to do homework.

Where did they think he'd be?

"Dude, I was just thinking about you!" Grinning broadly, Dylan looked up from his computer. "Saved me a trip. I was gonna ask you to check out my paper."

"Sure, sure," she stalled for time. "I've just gotta —" She glanced longingly at the bathroom door. "Um, wash up. You know, my hands are all . . . meat-loafy." That was all she could come up with.

Meat-loafy?! Even if she hadn't heard what Dylan was thinking, she could see it on his face. He thought she'd bugged.

"Yo," he said aloud, "you weren't eating with your hands. Anyway, what's wrong with the door on your side?"

"Lock blew off," she blurted. "I mean, the doorknob's stuck."

"Whatever." He couldn't care less. He had his own agenda. "Come on, Alex. It'll take a second. Just read this thing, okay?"

"I . . ." She cocked her head and listened for Cam's call, for any sign that it was time for her to rush back into their room.

Nothing.

Which figured.

She'd split only ten seconds ago.

The disguised clone thing that was trying to separate them probably needed a minute or two to regroup, to think of clever new nasties to turn them against each other.

"Okay. Just for a minute, though. I've got stuff of my own to do. So your paper?" Alex asked, ambling over to Dylan. "What's it on?"

* * *

It took all of ten seconds for Cam to feel the icy wind stream under the doorjamb. Shuddering, she forced herself to walk casually to her bed where the Coventry textbooks they'd used before dinner were collected. Her intention was to scoop them up and get them out of sight before Alex's clone entered — just in case the imp, who'd tossed the precious books into a trash bag last time, decided to do more damage to them.

She wasn't quick enough.

Her arms were full of books when the bogus twin burst into the room looking frighteningly Alex-like with a major grump on.

Cam stared hard at the girl, trying to find a crack, some flaw, a detail that was off, something to convince her it wasn't her twin she was facing.

"Yo, A-plus overachiever girl, what'd I tell you about messing with my books?"

If Cam hadn't known better, she'd have sworn it was her sister. The clone had Alex's snide-a-tude down pat.

"Bulletin, Als." Cam's voice sounded shaky even to her. "They're my books, too. Anyway, you're not going to need them, so what's your point?"

"My point is I want them." The creature, her nails the exact puke-green shade as Alex's, reached for the books.

66

"For what?" Cam challenged, pulling them out of range.

"I've gotta brush up on a couple of spells." The clone grinned maliciously. "I promised Cade I'd show him some real witchy tricks."

"No way," Cam shouted as if the real Alex had proposed something so dumb and dangerous. "You're not doing magick for Cade or anyone else we know —"

"Oh, I forgot," the imp said venomously, taking a step forward, her hands clawing for the books. "You and Cade are so cozy now that of course you'd know what would amuse him and what wouldn't —"

"It has nothing to do with Cade!" Cam insisted, hugging the pile of books and turning her back on the Alex imitator. Speaking of, where was her sister?

"Want to see some real magick?" the intruder asked.

Cam sent a telepathic SOS through the imaginary peephole. *Now, Alex. Shake it. She's here!*

Meanwhile, make-believe Alex's hands ripped a book from the stack Cam was holding. It was *The Little Book of Spells,* the one their guardian wanted them to memorize.

The grinning imposter opened the book and stared intently at one of its pages. An edge of the brittle paper began to crinkle and then blacken. Cam heard an almost imperceptible sound, a crackling that gave way to a curl of smoke. The mischievous sprite was burning Ileana's book!

Panicked, Cam tried to grab it back. *Alex, get in here, now!* she telegraphed.

Checking the imposter to see if she'd intercepted the call, Cam found herself staring into the girl's Alex-gray eyes.

No one she'd ever met anywhere, not even on Coventry, had those exact same eyes. Their birth mother Miranda's eyes and their cousin Ileana's were gray — but not the exact shade and intensity of Cam's. Or Alex's.

Lying eyes, Cam thought. And all at once, she knew what to do.

The Truth spell was one of the first she and Alex had tried together. They'd used it to instill trust in someone too frightened to tell the truth. Whether or not this Alex-looking creature was frightened, she *was* lying; she was hiding something. Cam glanced around the room. There was no time for her to gather the right herbs — burdock, chamomile, or lemon balm, she remembered. There was no time to dig in her jewelry basket for the rose quartz crystal that had once belonged to Karsh. There was no time to wait for Alex.

"*Oh, sun that brings us light and cheer, shine through me now to banish fear,*" she began the incantation. "*Free —*" She was supposed to use the person's name here, but she didn't know who stood before her. *"Free this fraud,"* she decided, *"from doubt and blame, win her trust and lift her shame."*

Nothing happened. Counterfeit Alex stood gaping at Cam.

"Okay." Cam took a breath. *Reveal, schlemiel, conceal . . .* She had it. *"Let me see through what she would conceal. Show me what she won't reveal. Put an end to this crazy game, that I may know who she is and why she came!"*

This time, the moment Cam stopped, the clone tried to cover her face. But it was too late. Cam saw her eyes, watched their color fade, their shape change.

Alex's eyes, identical to Cam's, were large and deep-set. The pretender's seemed shrunken suddenly, their vivid gray giving way to dull brown.

And the clothes her so-called sister was wearing were changing, too. Within the outline of Alex's body, a dark velvet robe appeared and disappeared. Like an object floating under a storm-tossed sea, the robe emerged, then sank beneath the jeans and T-shirt the clone had copied.

It was an optical illusion, Cam realized, one that she could only have witnessed with the help of the Truth spell. Amazing! She'd found a way to transform a human being without actually physically changing her. Alex's duplicate wasn't morphing. Thanks to the spell, Cam's view of her was! She was "seeing through" the impostor's disguise.

"I can do more than fry a book, sister," the strangely altered girl threatened. "Watch this!"

But Cam's powerful eyesight kicked into high gear, paralyzing her for a moment.

Instead of snatching back the precious book, from which a thin stream of smoke was rising, her attention was now riveted on the intruder's face.

Not *on* her face exactly, more like under it.

Stunned, she began to recognize the girl's subtly submerged features. . . .

Instinctively, Cam gripped her sun charm.

Alex gasped.

Dylan leaped up from his chair. "What?!" he asked, shaken.

She didn't answer. Her entire being was on alert. Listening.

The sound she heard was demanding, angry, distant. At first it droned like an enormous agitated bee from very far away.

Alex grew dizzy. Her head ached; her eyes closed. She began to make out words.

Sow confusion. Reap dissension. Tear them apart. Make each hate you — and thus each other.

The voice was deep, perversely delighted, and familiar.

It belonged to . . . ?

Alex's hand moved to her moon charm. It had begun to grow warm. She felt the gold amulet stir against her palm, felt it push forward as if drawn by a magnet.

Thantos!

She saw him. In the blackness behind her eyelids, she saw the hulking, bearded tracker talking to a robed young witch. The girl, whose hair was hidden by the hood of her cloak, was staring at him raptly. Alex could not see her face. But she could see her uncle's — spiteful, gleeful, malicious, determined. He was issuing orders.

He was commanding his underling . . . an apprentice witch who smelled of jimsonweed and nettle . . .

All at once, Alex knew who the girl was. Remembered her. Realized that Thantos, a tracker capable of transmutation, of changing human beings, was casting a spell over the creature.

He was ordering his treacherous servant to chip away at the twins, rip them apart, undermine them bit by bit.

Thantos took the urchin's shoulders and turned her

away from him. For a fleeting moment, Alex saw the girl's true face. And then it changed. It became hers! And Cam's. It was their bogus twin.

With great effort, Alex lifted her head and willed her eyes to open. Her skull was pounding. Her body was racked with chills. She knew the symptoms. She had seen Cam go through them often enough. But this time she was the one who'd had the vision. And it hadn't been a prophecy of the future. It was a picture from the very recent past.

"Yo, what's up?" Dylan was watching her, his eyes wide with fear and confusion. "Dude, what's happening to you?"

Alex's moon charm was red hot now. Suddenly, she heard Cam's silent cry: *Alex, where are you? I need help!*

"Alex," Dylan called to her, "say something. You're freaking me."

She hated to do it, but she had to.

Without herbs, without crystals, with nothing but her skill, her knowledge of the craft, and the amulet her father had forged for her, she recited the Lethe incantation.

A moment before Dylan fell into stupefied forgetfulness, she whispered to him, "Your paper rules, bro. Rest easy."

*   *   *

"It's Amaryllis!" Alex called, crashing into the bedroom she shared with her sister.

She'd half expected to find Cam in big trouble — singed by the Coventry witch's fiery gaze. But her twin was all right. It was the girl who looked exactly like Alex, down to the sheen of her black-dyed hair, who appeared to be in harm's way.

Wisps of smoke rose from the imposter's jeans and sweatshirt. Her face was smeared with soot as if she'd just crawled out of a chimney.

Clutching a smoldering book — Ileana's spell book! — Cam was glaring at the disheveled "Alex."

"It's really Amaryllis," Alex gushed. "I recognized her smell and then I saw her face. Cam, I had a vision!"

"Oh, really?" Cam asked, ticked that her twin had taken so long to pop in. "And who are you?"

"Me?" Alex said defensively. "Yo, I'm your sister, your one and only twin. And she's Uncle T"'s tool, Amaryllis."

"Prove it!" the smoke-damaged clone hollered from the floor.

Alex gave the girl a dirty look, then showed her sister her moon charm. "Camryn, it's me," she said, exasperated.

"Camryn, it's me!" her clone quickly echoed, scrambling to her feet. Mimicking Alex's frustrated cry, she pretended to grasp something at her throat.

But she was holding nothing. And Cam and Alex both knew it.

"Where were you?!" Cam demanded. "I've been trying to break through that dumbest-idea-of-the-decade 'door' of yours for five minutes!" The moment she said it, Cam realized her mistake. She'd forgotten to grasp her sun charm until the last minute.

"Well, I'm here now," Alex was saying, "and so is Uncle Thantos's latest messenger — emphasis on 'mess.' She was supposed to torch our books and make you think I was doing it. He wanted to turn us against each other again —"

"Give me news, not history," Cam responded. "She started the fire, but I got it to ricochet, to blaze backward. I can't believe he's still pulling the same old tricks. Trying to split us up. He's tried it how many times now? Three just with Shane —"

"See, you can't blame me then, can you?" Amaryllis, still in her charred Alex incarnation, argued shrewdly. "I mean, I'm only one of his lackeys, just like Shane."

"I am so not interested in Shane Wright," Cam said too quickly.

Just as quickly, Amaryllis's eyes, still flashing between gray and brown, lit up with new mischief.

"Shane A. Wright? Good thing, too. Since the buff boy is so not interested in *you*. Never was," Alex's replica declared. "It was me — I mean, Alex — all the time. You're too spoiled and perfect. So the good girl. And talk about clueless! You bought everything Shane said. I guess you never got it, I mean how Alex was always more his type —"

"Just like Cade's all crushed on Cam, right?" Alex challenged the malicious girl. "I'd say 'nice try,' but 'pathetic last attempt' is more like it."

But Amaryllis had hit her target — Cam's heart. Alex had heard her sister's gasp, saw her quick tears spring up.

"Don't go there. She's lying," Alex warned Cam, forgetting to send rather than say the message. "She's just doing what Thantos trained her to do —"

"Sure I am," Amaryllis insisted. "And I'll use anything to do it — even the truth! Which reminds me, Camryn — remember Jason, the boy who would be boyfriend, your true-blue high school biscuit who's at college now? He's not all that wild about you anymore, either —"

"Shut up," Alex ordered.

"Or what? You'll use your famous telekinetic beam to bean me . . . with, say —" The girl surveyed the room. Her eyes lighted on the massive *Morphing and Transformation Handbook* on Cam's bed. "— that book. Go on. Use your supposedly awesome glare for something other than gaping at me. Let's see you make that sucker rise up and strike me!"

"Don't!" Cam shouted, grabbing Alex's shirttail as she spun toward the bed. "She's just trying to get you to do something hateful. Something to mess up our viewing!"

"Aren't you the clever twin?" Amaryllis mocked. "Grab a crayon and take notes, Alex. You're kinda slow compared to Cam. She is so the pop princess. And so boringly always right. Oh, by the way, princess, your mom is definitely planning an at-home get-together for your birthday. A totally ho-hum dillyo. Ten people for supper. Supper!" She turned to Alex. "Guess that means you'll be celebrating your sixteenth with the celebrated Six Pack. Oh, yeah, and Em's doing the cooking! Isn't that too cool? You're in for a treat, one of her inedible barf-inducing specials! Guess the post-dinner festivities will be a spew fest. A fabulous night to remember."

"No way!" Cam shouted. Then added less surely, "She wouldn't."

Alex turned toward the bed again as if she were going to telepathically hoist and lob the book across the room at the troublemaker. To add authenticity to the threat, she focused on the thick volume forcing it to fly up into her hand.

"Stop!" Amaryllis hollered. And when Alex faced her, the girl stuck out her Alex chin and said, "I mean, it's your Initiation month. Vengefulness, unjust punishment, bullying a lesser witch — which I am; I'm not even scheduled for Initiation yet — all that is totally frowned upon. Big time. It'll cost you major stones. You don't want to foul up your viewing by doing anything sleazy to me."

"Cam might not," Alex said, letting the handbook drop and hoping the door to her thoughts was still locked, "but since I'm not going back to Coventry, I've got nothing to lose, have I?"

Her impersonator studied her, trying to make out whether she was serious or not. And then, as clearly as if she'd spoken them aloud, Amaryllis's thoughts became transparent to Alex.

If Alex was telling the truth, then at least part of her mission was successful, the clone mused. She'd kept one twin from being initiated!

But would that be enough? Would it satisfy her demanding master?

It had to, Alex heard the girl tell herself. Hadn't Lord Thantos said that stopping one of them would cut their skill and strength in half?

Despite the bluster, Amaryllis had begun to tremble.

As she heard the witch's desperate thoughts and read the fear in her eyes, Alex's anger began to cool. In its place came an unexpected pang of regret. She felt — what was it?

Shame.

The emotion floored her, flooded her. She felt ashamed at having fooled the frightened clone into believing that she was going to skip out on her Initiation. Amaryllis was counting on it, hoping that it would appease their vicious uncle.

Wisdom, intuition, trust, courage, and honesty. The virtues on which she and Cam were being judged came back to her. She'd definitely lapsed on honesty. And probably trust. And what kind of courage did it take to taunt a terrified servant?

She was about to confess the lie to Amaryllis when the arrogant young witch dismissed her with a wave of her hand and a smile of pure malice. "Good idea. Skip the trip. Totally nothing to lose," she assured Alex.

And then, as if she'd suddenly realized that Alex could read her thoughts, Amaryllis quickly scrambled them — and moved on to the next ploy.

"You know why Cade *pretends* to care about you? Because he pities you! Like, who wouldn't? Talk about a raw deal. While Cam was being fed with a silver spoon, you were pitifully scraping peanut butter out of a jar. She got to keep both of her adoptive parents — and you got to be an orphan! And weren't you the manipulating babe to spill all that to Cade?" The vixen turned to Cam. "She totally smeared you!"

Alex shook her head. "Not," she told her sister. "The snake's just doing her job."

"Right you are." Amaryllis jumped on it. "This con wasn't my idea. It's strictly a family affair. I'm just your uncle's gofer. Just trying to do him a favor. Don't murder the messenger, okay?"

Cam ignored her. "This is too weird," she told her sister. "How do we get her out of that whack getup?"

"What are you saying?" Alex wanted to know. "She looks like me. What's whack about that?"

"Okay, not whack, just confusing," Cam back-pedaled. "I keep flashing between what she really looks like and this creepy version of you."

"Wire your uncle," Amaryllis suggested sarcastically. "He did this, he can undo it. And believe me, it was no day at the beach being either of you." She held up her hands, making talking gestures with them, opening and closing her fingers like bird beaks. "Bicker, bicker, bicker," she said.

"I've had it." Cam turned her back on the smoke-smeared imitation of Alex and pretended more anger than she felt. "Let's get this over with. What should we do with her?"

She touched her sun charm and saw that Alex had caught the move and held her moon amulet now. *Like*

really, what are we going to do with her? Cam posed the question through the peephole to her twin. *Should we just run a Traveler's spell on her and send her back exactly as she is?*

Alex's quick answer surprised her. *Too harsh. The bravado is strictly bogus. It's all an act. Check it out yourself. She's scared stiff.*

Check it out? Her thoughts are scrambled, Cam sent back. But *could* she tune in to Amaryllis? she wondered.

Ileana had told them that their powers would take extreme turns now. They'd be able to do more than ever before — and, just as unpredictably, tank. During this sacred time, their gifts could peak suddenly or plummet.

It seemed to be happening — the upswing, anyway. Alex had done an awesome Einstein on the door-and-peephole idea. And Cam had come up with the right incantation to see through her sister's look-alike. Plus she was getting good at picking up unspoken thoughts.

She focused in on Amaryllis again, this time with her eyes *and* her ears.

Colors danced inside her closed eyelids. Bright, almost blinding lines that reminded Cam of spilled paint running in a hundred directions at once — streaming, bubbling, exploding.

She concentrated harder, listened more intensely,

and became aware of noise — crackling, spitting, swirling sounds that accompanied the jerky movements of the painfully bright lines. The churning static began to sound like . . . disconnected words . . . fragments of phrases.

Suddenly, Cam's head swam with the frightened but defiant young witch's desperate thoughts.

A sentence broke through the senseless clamor: *How am I going to get out of this?*

And then another: *What's Lord Thantos going to do to me?! He's already told me there's no going back. I'm stuck in this look for at least a month!*

And then she heard: *They're supposed to be so excellently ethical and devoted to the Coventry creed —*

Amaryllis was thinking of them, Cam realized, of her and Alex.

Maybe they'd treat me — not with forgiveness exactly. That would take more mercy than fledglings are usually capable of — but maybe . . . compassion?

Fat chance, Amaryllis decided. The racket grew loud again. Cam barely heard: *How can I soften them up? What do I have to bargain with?*

The cornered girl brightened suddenly. A single word rose above the clatter of fear and desperation in her mind. Cam glanced quickly at Alex to see whether she'd heard it, too.

"Shane," Alex said.

"Shane again," Cam noted, disappointed.

"You guys are good," Amaryllis acknowledged. "It's not what you think. Shane, yes. Old news, no. Remember how you said, 'Give me news, not history'? Well, this is the genuine dish." She lifted two fingers in a V. "Witch's honor."

"Let's hear it," Alex said skeptically.

"First let me get this straight. You," Amaryllis said to her, "are definitely *not* going back to Coventry. No Initiation for you. Have I got that right?"

"Not exactly," Alex murmured.

Amaryllis turned white.

"The scoop on Shane," Cam demanded.

"What about *me*?" Amaryllis moaned. "I can't go home now. Not with your uncle knowing I botched it. It's bad enough that my transmutation can't be reversed even on Coventry, that I've gotta stay in my twin-skin for a whole month. Now I'm going to have to hang out in dork world looking like you!"

"Maybe not," Alex said. She did, after all, owe the girl something.

"But first you've got to spill your Shane secret," Cam cut in.

Amaryllis checked them out. "Trust is one of the virtues you're going to be viewed on," she reminded them. "If I trust you, you better not betray me —"

"Deal," Alex agreed.

"Dish," Cam said.

"Well, for starters," their clone began cautiously, "he is not what you think. I mean, you believe he's loyal to Lord Thantos, right?"

Cam nodded.

"Nuh-uh," Amaryllis crooned, sounding embarrassingly like her, Cam thought. "Shane A. Wright is not a fan of your uncle's. There is no love lost between his family and yours, trust me."

"His family? But his parents threw him out when he turned against Thantos," Cam pointed out.

"Nuh-uh," Amaryllis said again.

"Could you not do that?" Cam asked.

"Go on," Alex urged. "You were saying something about Shane's family —"

"What's in it for me?" Amaryllis wanted to know.

Cam and Alex looked at each other.

"Safe passage back to Coventry," Cam offered.

"And I'll keep up the pretense," Alex promised, "that I'm a no-show for the last leg of our Initiation. At least until you can pack your bags and get out of Crailmore."

"That way no one will know your trip was a washout. How's that?" Cam asked.

After a moment's consideration and a searching look at their faces, Amaryllis continued with relish. "Okay.

Here's the dirt. Shane's parents? Supposed to have dumped him? Never happened. They just keep a low profile — and for good reason. They don't want any DuBaer thinking that their son wants to get next to Big T — which your old pal Shane's been trying to do for years and years. It's almost embarrassing how the boy sucks up to your uncle. But Lord Thantos doesn't, repeat does not, trust Shane A. Wright."

"Thantos doesn't trust anybody," Cam noted.

Amaryllis shrugged. "Hey, I haven't been initiated yet so maybe my instincts are whack. But if your unc has a special place in his heart for Shane, trust me, it's in the deepest, darkest, bloodiest chamber."

"But why?" Cam asked, then shuddered as much at the wickedly triumphant look suddenly lighting Amaryllis's face as at her sinister words.

"Whoops! That's a no-no!" the Coventry witch gloated. "You know the rules. I can't answer any of your questions during your Initiation month. But you can answer one of mine. How am I getting home?"

CHAPTER EIGHT
WISDOM AND INTUITION

They were wiped out.

The Traveler's spell had not been as easy as they'd imagined. They'd performed it before, but only to transport *themselves*. Achieving liftoff for Amaryllis turned out to be more difficult. And having her hanging around was even worse.

Thantos's little accomplice whined and jeered at their every failed attempt to get rid of her. It was nearly midnight before they hit on the right combination of words, stones, herbs, and, most important, attitudes. It turned out they needed to be positive. Only when they were too worn out to waste time or energy on annoyance, anger, frustration, or any other negative thought or emotion, did the spell work. Amaryllis split Marble Bay shortly after twelve.

She was there complaining about their lack of will and skill at 12:04; at 12:05, without so much as a buh-bye, she was gone. By then neither Cam nor Alex was up for a gab session; sleep and silence were what they'd both craved.

But they struck out on both counts.

Cam tossed and turned and stared up at the street-light-lit tree shadows dancing on the ceiling while her mind rambled relentlessly. The convo in her head went back and forth between two subjects: Shane and sweet sixteen.

Okay, Shane had told a lie about being cast out by his family. No biggie. Lying was what the boy did best. Believing his lies was her specialty, Cam mused ruefully.

But how was his family involved? That was the newsy part of Amaryllis's trade-in. According to Thantos's hench-witch, Shane's family, the Wrights, cared about what the DuBaers thought. Not what Thantos thought, but the DuBaers, Amaryllis had specified.

Whatever Shane hoped to gain by winning their vicious uncle's trust would apparently affect his whole family.

Why would Shane's parents not want *any* DuBaer to

know that their son was trying to get on the good side of Thantos?

Was there some kind of family feud going on between the Wrights and the DuBaers? A dark family secret? Another family curse?

The Antayus curse was the only one she and Alex knew about. Lord Karsh had described it in his final journal.

It had originated hundreds of years ago when one of their ancestors, the physician Jacob DuBaer, had grown jealous of a beloved healer named Abigail Antayus. A secret warlock himself, Jacob ratted Abigail out to the witch hunters of Salem.

After her capture and terrible death, Abigail's son vowed that in every generation an Antayus would bring about the death of a DuBaer — specifically, the leader of the clan, who for generations had always been the eldest DuBaer son.

In all the years that followed, the curse had never failed to come true.

As he lay dying, Cam and Alex's grandfather Nathaniel devised a way to end the bloodshed. He decided that he should be the last male to lead the family. After his death, only females who were immune to the curse would rule.

That accounted for what everyone called the twins'

destiny. They were females. They were DuBaers. They were supposed to rule. After Initiation.

The Antayus curse was scary enough, Cam thought. Were there other curses and grievances waiting for them on Coventry?

Frustrated, she had punched her pillow and rolled over again. As if she'd flipped an index card, the next topic assailed her.

"Supper for ten," she thought, her heart sinking. And Emily, who was so not the master chef, was going to prepare the feast herself. No crowd. No caterers. A sit-down meal for ten. That'd be Em, Dave, Dylan, the Six Pack, and . . . Cam and Alex would make it eleven, not ten.

Alex wasn't going to show! That was it! She must have somehow let Emily know she wasn't interested in coming to her own birthday party. . . . Which, of course, had to mean that Alex had come clean with Em and confessed that they knew, both of them, that there was a bash brewing.

No. She couldn't have. She wouldn't have.

Then what was Amaryllis talking about? Or was she just "sowing dissension" — finding ways to confuse and conquer — as Thantos had programmed her to do?

Well, if it was confusion the Coventry witch had been trying to promote, she'd succeeded. Cam was thoroughly confused now. And too wound up to sleep.

And there was no one to talk about it with. Her twin hadn't moved or made a peep since lights-out. How could Alex sleep at a time like this?

"Sleep?!" Alex had unexpectedly declared. "Not with you yammering. Mute the mind-muttering, would you? I've got issues of my own!"

"Like what?" Cam had asked eagerly, sitting up and snapping on the light.

"Shut that off!" Alex had ordered. "I'm trying to get some Z's."

She was.

Trying.

And failing. When *were* they supposed to return to Coventry for their final tests and actual Initiation ceremony? she'd been wondering. On their last visit to the island, both Ileana and Miranda had been vague about it. Sometime during their birthday month, was all they'd say.

And all Rhianna had said was, "You will be called at the auspicious moment."

Auspicious? Favorable, lucky, promising . . . When was that supposed to be? When the sun was at its zenith? When the moon was in the seventh house? Could they have been less specific?

Sun and moon! The excited thought was Cam's, playing off Alex's unspoken question.

Of course!

They'd been born when both the sun and moon were in the sky — Alex just as the full moon was fading, Cam minutes later as the sun rose.

"It'll be at the full moon!" Cam turned the light back on. "Like when we were born!"

"What are you doing?" Alex whined.

"Looking at the calendar," Cam answered, racing to her desk. "Full moon in October . . . ?" She pounded the calendar page with her forefinger. "It falls on the sixteenth! O.M.G., that's like, two weeks away!"

"Ya think?" It was Alex's turn to punch a pillow. Which she did and turned her back on her sister. "Shut the light!"

The cafeteria was noisy and crowded the next day at lunchtime. Alex was already there when Cam walked in. Alex and Cade were sharing a table with Dylan and the boardies, most of them done up in baggies, knee-length shirts, and knit caps riding low on their brows. Neither Cam nor Alex had gotten much sleep the night before — and their minds were still on Amaryllis.

Beth and Bree were at their usual place, Cam saw. Beth was munching tuna salad in a pita, while Bree was checking out a veggie burger, peering under the bun to be sure not a scrap of beef had slipped past the steam table police.

Behind them, two tables away, same as yesterday, Nadine Somerfeld sat alone. Cam hoped the new girl would look up so she could smile or nod at her or maybe walk over and say hi. But the vibe coming off Nadine was tense and defensively "I'm cool alone."

She was focusing intently on . . . Cam telescoped in on the book the new girl was staring at . . . a social studies textbook. But she hadn't turned the page — and Cam could see that her eyes were not moving, not following the text. Nadine wasn't really reading, she was just trying to look engrossed.

As she headed for the Six Pack table, Cam's thoughts turned away from her Amaryllis-inspired angst and she felt a rush of sympathy for the nervous newcomer. There was something touching and familiar about Nadine's loneliness and her attempt to cover it up. Obviously, she cared about what other people thought of her. The book was clearly a prop. But she was doing her best to cope, to pretend she was totally independent and importantly occupied.

She reminded Cam of Alex. And of herself. Before she and Alex had connected, Cam had done her share of pretending. She was popular, made the honor roll year after year, was always picked first for a team — but inside, she had felt as lonely as Nadine looked. And as nervous, always worrying that someone would find out how weird she was.

"She is. She's just weird."

The sinister whisper startled Cam. It had come from the Six Pack table . . . where Bree was arguing with Beth about . . . Nadine.

"She's not weird," Beth insisted. "She's just new —"

"Whatever," Bree cut her off. "I am not inviting her to sit with us. Hey," she said as Cam set down her tray. "Beth's having a charity moment for Nerd-ine."

"Stop calling her that," Beth hissed.

"You are so hypocritical," Bree shot back. "Yesterday you were all, 'Ooooh, she's so Salvation Army —'"

"That is not what I said. I just meant —"

Cam didn't want a piece of the debate. Maybe it was because she was so tired, or maybe it was because she didn't want to sound holier than Bree.

Bree, Cam knew, was the princess of pretending to be cool. Her family situation was a disaster. Her mom had never gotten over the divorce; her father had never gotten over himself. The two of them were so caught up in their own war that Bree was basically a combat casualty hanging on by a thread.

Cam had known Bree, and the rest of the Six Pack, since grade school. Even back then, Bree was kind of a mess. "Compare and Contrast Waxman," they used to tease her because that's what she did all the time. "Do you think my . . ." — fill in the blank: hair, nose, clothes, height, weight — ". . . is better than hers?" It was sad but true that, too often, only by making people think less of someone could Bree think more of herself.

Still, it was an annoying, sometimes infuriating trait. And basically played out, Cam thought. They were all sixteen or about to be. It was time for Bree to grow up.

"Private clash or can anyone jump in?" Kristen, Bree's best friend, waited for Beth to move her backpack from the chair next to Bree.

Beth complied. "Your BFF is ragging on Nadine again," she grumbled.

"Nerd-ine," Bree corrected her.

Even Kristen rolled her eyes at the childish jab.

"Oh, no." Beth sounded even more upset. "That's all she needs now!"

Cam followed Beth's gaze and saw "Skeevy Stevie" Hitchens heading for the new girl's table. Usually the beefy bully sat alone, throwing his jacket over one chair, dropping his backpack on another, hogging as much of the table as he could, and scaring off anyone who tried to sit down with him.

As he approached Nadine's table, holding a full tray — supersized soda, french fries with ketchup, and a large bowl of chili — he started to pretend to be slipping and sliding as if he were going to fall.

Cam didn't need a prophetic vision to know what

would happen next. Every bit of slop on his tray was going to wind up on Nadine's oblivious head. The bully especially enjoyed tormenting Nadine.

Alex caught it, too. Instantly, she telegraphed Cam, *Okay, I can reverse the tray and make it dump food all over Skeevy Stevie or you can dazzle him into falling backward. Either way, he's wearing lunch.*

Hold that thought, Cam responded, *and try this one.* An idea had come to her. A total inspiration! Except that it required ingredients that would be impossible to find here and now.

Like a daisy. And a nugget of silver.

The precious metal had a strangely specific power. It could make someone appreciate the purity and simplicity of poverty. Silver. Cam zeroed in on Beth's turquoise-and-silver bracelet. Maybe that would work.

But a daisy? The flower was excellent for relieving stress — particularly the kind of stress that could hide the simplicity of a heart. Where was she going to find a daisy in October? She and Alex had dried some, along with a dozen other useful flowers, last summer. But they were at home in a bowl on her dresser! She could call up a picture of the flower in her mind, she guessed. It was worth a try.

Now if only she could remember the chant for turning a negative into a positive — the If-you've-got-a-lemon-make-lemonade spell, Ileana had called it.

Through the power of these elements, let change be done, Alex remembered the beginning of the incantation and sent it to Cam.

Hang on, Cam sent back. "Bree," she said aloud, "do you think Beth's bracelet is real silver?"

"Huh?" Beth and Bree said together.

"Just wondering." Cam tried to sound casual.

"Let me see that," Bree ordered Beth.

"No way." Beth started to pull her hand away, which was all the incentive Bree needed to grab hold of her wrist. The moment Bree touched the silver band, a bouquet of daisies sprouted in Cam's mind. She could practically smell their sweet earthy fragrance.

Through the power of these elements, let change be done, she silently recited. *Where once there was evil, now harm none. Where once there was darkness, now shine a light. That Bree may seek what is just, what is right. Let her see goodness where before she saw ill. With loving-kindness may her heart fill.*

"Poor Skeevy Stevie," Bree suddenly announced. "He is so the insecure show-off."

Oh, no, Cam thought. *She's shining her light on the wrong customer.*

But a nanosecond later, Bree added, "I'm not gonna sit here and let him hurt Nadine just 'cause he's hurting."

Kristen and Beth watched goggle-eyed as Bree, tiny and determined, stomped across the lunchroom, shoved the snickering, tray-clutching bully out of the way, and invited a very startled, very grateful Nadine to join her at the Six Pack table.

Kudos and congrats, Camo! Alex memoed her sister.

"Hey!" Thwarted and confused, Stevie hollered after the girls, "Whaddya do that for?"

The jeering laughter around him took him by surprise. His face reddened darkly as he spun away from Bree and Nadine to scowl at the lunch bunch taunting him. His grip on the overloaded tray became so tight that his knuckles whitened. He was shaking with rage.

Make that humiliation and embarrassment, Alex realized, studying the boy.

He was a bully and a clown and undoubtedly deserved to be treated with contempt, to be laughed at and rejected. But his defeat was hard to watch.

Especially since, without warning, Alex seemed to be seeing through his eyes!

As if she'd inhabited Skeevy Stevie's skin and was looking out, Alex saw the kids in the lunchroom laughing and pointing, calling out insults, and, worst of all, rolling their eyes in disgust or, with a wave of their hands, dismissing him. Only it felt as if it were happening to her.

And it hurt. She could feel her chest tighten, her heart begin to race. With each quickened pulse, tears pushed up out of some bottomless pit of sorrow in her gut.

She was literally feeling *his* pain.

As if from far away, she could hear Dylan saying, "Yo, forget him."

Which was what everyone now seemed to be doing. They went about their business — eating, talking, laughing, shouting, and pointedly ignoring Stevie.

Shaken, Alex's mind returned to the body she'd left sitting beside Cade at the skateboarding slackers' table. From there she watched Stevie making his way out of the lunchroom, head down, shoulders slumping.

"Feel like a walk?" Cade asked, picking up his tray and pushing back from the table.

"Sure," Alex said uncertainly.

"They've sent the imposter back," Miranda happily reported to Rhianna.

"And bonus," Ileana declared, "they did it with kindness, compassion, justice, and love!"

Rhianna frowned at the twins' keyed-up guardian.

"Okay, scratch the love part and add that they did it

after one failed attempt," Ileana acquiesced, tossing her head and flinging back a cascade of shimmering blond curls. "But certainly they showed amazing compassion and kindness. And they learned from their mistake."

Rhianna was not in the best of moods. They'd buttonholed her as she was leaving her home. She'd been on her way to the Village Plaza, indeed had been looking forward to meeting Lady Fan there for an early-bird dinner, and did not welcome the interruption. "And this surprises you?" she asked curtly.

"Of course not," Miranda said.

"Hello." Ileana rolled her eyes. "It's the first week of their Initiation and they just handled a completely unsanctioned situation superbly. They used wisdom . . ." She held up her thumb. "Intuition . . ." She added her forefinger. Then stopped, frustrated. "Come on, Rhianna. Be fair. Smoking out Amaryllis and then finding a way to help the evil little imp escape Thantos's wrath has got to be worth big points!"

"For most fledglings, yes," Rhianna agreed, reluctantly pushing back the door to her cottage and leading her surprise guests inside. "But of Artemis and Apolla, one expects no less."

"So they're being punished for being brighter than other fledglings?" Ileana complained. "What?!" she added as the twins' mother kicked her.

Miranda's attempt to caution the rash young witch pleased Rhianna. A smile twitched at the corners of her mouth as she led them to the glass-front cupboard that held Cam's and Alex's viewing boxes.

Each gold container was inscribed with the girls' Coventry names under the crowned bear crest of the DuBaer family. There was an opening in the shape of a pentagram, a five-sided star, at the top of each box.

As Lady Rhianna unlocked the cabinet, Miranda's hand reached toward the containers, as if by touching them she could touch again their maker. It was Aron, her murdered husband, father of the twins, who had crafted the boxes, as he had their daughters' sun and moon charms, in the days before their birth.

Out of the corner of her eye, Rhianna caught the gesture. She removed the boxes carefully, one at a time, and handed the first to Miranda. Then, so as not to embarrass Aron's widow, and to appear evenhanded, she gave the second box to the twins' impulsive, tactless, and, most bewilderingly, Karsh-appointed guardian, Ileana.

In a golden bowl on the shelf above the viewing boxes were sparkling crystals and precious and semiprecious stones of every shape and color. Rhianna dipped her plump hand into the bowl and drew out a fistful of stones.

"Apolla deserves at least three points for intuition, for flushing out Amaryllis," Ileana declared.

"Artemis as well. They both treated the girl with compassion," Miranda reminded her daughters' Initiation Master.

"For uncovering not only who, but why —" Rhianna began, trying to ignore them.

"At least two points for wisdom, then. Two stones, surely," Miranda broke in.

"And courage," Ileana said. "It took great courage and even trust!"

"Courage certainly deserves several points. Don't you think?" Miranda asked Rhianna.

The old witch rolled her eyes in exasperation. "The boxes," she demanded.

Ileana and Miranda held them at arm's length. With mind-boggling speed, Rhianna picked a number of stones from her hand and deposited them into the containers.

The *plink-clink, click-clack* of pebbles hitting thick gold pleased Miranda, though neither she nor Ileana had been sharp enough to see how many stones the old witch had awarded nor into whose boxes they'd been dropped.

"Listen up," Rhianna curtly commanded. "This is how it is. For waylaying the bully in the cafeteria, Apolla earns two stones. For feeling the bad boy's pain, three for Artemis. For working together, two more each. And for gloating —" Rhianna upended the boxes and shook a stone out of each — "that's a minus two."

After returning the boxes and bowl to her cupboard, Rhianna hurried to her door. Grabbing Miranda's hand, Ileana rushed to catch up with the Exalted Elder. "One more thing," she called out.

"I think not." Rhianna quickened her pace, leaving the door to her cottage ajar. "Not now. You've already taken too much of my time."

"Time is just the issue!" Ileana chased after the quick-striding witch.

"What the child means," Miranda intervened, "is we were wondering *when* you're planning to convene the Initiation?"

Rhianna hurried on. "The thirtieth and the thirty-first, of course," she huffed, without turning around or slowing down.

"But —" Miranda called after her. Ileana released her hand and raced ahead, holding up the hem of her midnight-blue gown.

"Wait up, your esteemed eminence," the twins' guardian called as respectfully as she could manage. Politeness did not trip easily off her tongue. But if ever there was a time to catch flies with honey, this was it. "Lady Rhianna, I've been thinking —"

"Always a dangerous thing!" With a huge sigh, Rhianna whirled to face the women.

"No, really — why must their forty-eight hours have

to be the day before and the day of their birth dates?" Ileana continued, "Why not hold the Initiation at the full moon, as Apolla believes it will be? You know that their mainland family is planning a gala celebration for their birthday —"

"Rhianna, dear friend." Miranda joined the fight. "Why not honor their adoptive parents by allowing the party to take place as planned?"

"They are already honored by having been chosen to rear extraordinary children," Rhianna said curtly.

Ileana shook her head. "You don't understand. You just don't get it! Emily, the mother, has gone to such pains —"

Rhianna's large downy wings bristled as if preparing to unfurl. "Enough!" she commanded. "The DuBaer twins are bright and resourceful enough to meet any challenge put before them. They must be!"

"And so they are," Miranda asserted. "You are right, of course. They'll find a way to deal with the situation." She turned to see how Ileana was taking the rebuff.

But Ileana's focus had shifted. *Someday I'll have wings like those,* she mused, staring at Lady Rhianna. *Or maybe not,* she decided unhappily, since they were granted only to those who had been of extraordinary service to the community.

And really, what had she done to deserve such marvelous appendages? Nothing of merit. She'd merely acted as a mentor to Cam and Alex. Which had been easy given how intelligent, talented, and teachable they were.

Lady Rhianna was watching her, waiting.

"All right, point taken," Ileana said with rare humility. "It was insolent of me to suggest bending the rules. That's what ruffled your feathers, isn't it?"

Lady Rhianna seemed taken aback. "Well, well, well," was all she could say as she studied the beautiful and vain young witch who had given away her childhood to care for and protect Apolla and Artemis.

Over the next week, Alex and Cam practiced their magick at every op. Never before had they been so tuned in to the various problems of their classmates and peers. The knowledge of their "viewing" made them take notice. It was totally empowering.

Her sight now nearly as good as her phenomenal hearing, Alex shielded Dylan from a stealth trip-up attack by Caroline Ledbetter. The freshman girl's unrequited crush on Dyl had turned to anger. The "Astral Glow" Alex sent had surrounded Dylan with a blinding burst of light — which kept Caroline from seeing her quarry, let alone sticking out her foot and sending him sprawling headfirst into the cafeteria trash can.

When an unprepared Beth got called on to stand

and deliver in Biology, Cam tried a telepathic forwarding spell. By sending her best friend a visual of a random man in one of those *Save The* T-shirts, Beth blurted out, "Manatee," the correct response to a question about an endangered sea mammal typically found in the southern hemisphere.

With way too much studying to do, Alex considered casting a spell to make her English teacher forget to give out homework. In the end, she decided against it. Mrs. Conner was one of those passionate types who loved what she taught and was more stoked than her students when a kid really "got" a poem or story or essay. Alex opted against less homework in favor of not messing with Mrs. Conner's teaching plan or her head.

Cam came up against a different moral dilemma. A player from the Salem Wildcats, Marble Bay's toughest opposing team, was having a miserable game and getting hammered more by her own ticked-off teammates than by Cam's peeps. Desperate and defeated, the girl stood between Cam and an easy goal.

Cam's competitive nature wanted to win both the game and the gratitude of her pumped-up teammates. To kick the goal or kick the girl's self-esteem up a notch? A split-second decision gave the edge to compassion over competition. Cam purposely blew the shot.

And when Cam saw eyes roll as Briana described

her father's "fabulous" last visit — a trip Cam knew had been another brutal no-show — she laid a Truth spell on her bud. The magick got Bree to confess to what really happened: Her dad had chosen a Caribbean cruise over his promised visit to his daughter — and had caught a mystery ailment that had all the passengers barfing their way back home. Bree and her audience totally cracked up over the props payback.

On October thirteenth, Alex aided hapless Hannah Priestly, the least-talented girl in math class. During a math team contest, Alex guided the girl's hand to write on the blackboard *DM,* as the correct abbreviation for Decimal, while her teammates incorrectly wrote *DC,* or *DEC.* Alex glowed when the teacher said, "Only one of you is correct," and Hannah looked around cluelessly. The teacher said her name, and her teammates rushed her and raised her high in the air, as if she'd just won the World Series.

Becoming a full-fledged witch was going to have its extremely cool moments, Alex thought.

And then, without warning, an image of Stevie Hitchens crossed her mind. A snapshot of how she'd seen him last — a sorry, slumped figure slinking out of the cafeteria. The utter opposite of the amazed and ecstatic Hannah.

* * *

Wisdom.

At home that afternoon, Cam decided to look up the word.

Alex came into their room and caught her flipping through the big dictionary. "What're you trying to find?" she asked, proud of her vocabulary know-how, her language skills. She could probably help Cam with any definition she needed. She was a writer, after all. Well, a songwriter anyway.

Cam jumped at the question as if she'd been caught doing something smarmy.

"Nothing. Um. Just something. You know, just curious . . ."

But Alex was already at her shoulder, peering at the open page, which began with the word *wide-awake* and ended with *wild bergamot.* "Wild bergamot's a purple-flowering plant." She couldn't help showing off — courtesy of two hours of ferocious cramming with *The Coventry Catalog of Herbs and Sundry Flora.*

"No. I was just checking out —"

"*Wisdom,*" Alex read her mind and jumped in. "Wisdom? Why?"

"I was just wondering whether the episode with Bree and Nadine fell under wisdom or intuition — or for that matter, trust, courage, or honesty," Cam confessed, sounding frustrated.

"You're grading yourself!" Alex laughed. "Why am I so not shocked? I mean, who but a control freak like you would have to figure out —"

"What points I earned? Hello, who but me has a right to know?" Cam responded heatedly. "Anyway, here's what it says. Do you want to know?"

"The business with Amaryllis," Alex said, "I figure that was intuition, big time. Plus a dab of honesty and maybe even trust on my part, since I 'fessed up about getting initiated —"

"I know. I gave you points for that," Cam said.

"Excuse me? You're grading me, too?!"

"Chill, Alex. So far you're doing okay. Here it is. Listen to this. 'Wisdom: having the power of discerning and judging properly what is true or right; showing such power . . .' blah, blah, blah . . . 'to make or to become aware or enlightened.' O.M.G.!" Cam paused, surprised. "Listen to this. The last meaning. It's labeled archaic — as in ancient, old-fashioned, outdated. 'Having knowledge of magic or witchcraft!'"

"That'd be us." Alex announced, "So we've aced wisdom on all counts."

Just then, once again, Stevie Hitchens crossed her mind. "Kind of," she amended, no longer smiling.

"By the way, know what today is?" Cam asked, shutting the dictionary.

"Tuesday," Alex answered flatly.

"The thirteenth!"

"And this news should shake me because?" Alex prompted.

"Hello. Three days to the full moon, remember?" Cam said. "We should be getting the call to Coventry anytime now."

That being the case, Alex thought, she had some quick and serious work to do on Stevie Hitchens.

CHAPTER NINE
THE CALL

Friday the sixteenth came and went. The full moon had shone gloriously into their room. And while Alex slept, Cam had sat up at the edge of her bed, fully dressed — in one of her favorite cashmere sweater sets — determinedly waiting for the call.

It never came.

And then another Friday — the twenty-third — rolled by. And still no word from Coventry.

Cam and Alex had continued to cram. They had memorized and practiced some awesome spells at home and at school. They'd created new incantations, most of which worked surprisingly well. Their talents were definitely improving — particularly Cam's mind-reading ability. As for hunches and premonitions, Alex had experienced at least three, counting the one in Dylan's room when she'd seen Amaryllis's face.

Stressed out by waiting, Cam had tried to figure out how their viewing might be going. She doled out points to herself . . . and to Alex. By her reckoning, they were neck and neck now.

But a week ago her twin had bounded into the lead with a single act of trust and courage. She'd befriended Stevie Hitchens.

And gotten him to apologize to Nadine.

With whom he fell in love!

Now the two of them held hands in the hallways and neither the new girl nor the bully sat alone at lunch anymore.

Alex swore she'd used no magic to accomplish this. She'd done nothing but hide a topaz stone in Stevie's backpack — topaz being a gem of courage, excellent for dispelling fear and insecurity with the light and warmth of love.

Cam had caught up to her sister just days ago. And it was Beth who'd provided the opportunity.

All of a sudden, Cam's laid-back best was obsessing about a business trip her mom was supposed to take. The trip itself was a week away. It had never been a big deal before. Now Beth couldn't let go of it. She kept saying she felt lonely already. And — as if it were the most brilliant idea she'd ever had — how cool would it be if Cam and, okay, Alex, too, bunked in with her?

It wasn't even what she said that was off, but the way she said it. Overstoked, hyper, practically giggling — all very un-Beth.

After soccer practice one afternoon, Cam suggested they split a pie at PITS. By then she was sure something was up.

Her tall, gangly, curly-haired bud was beyond up for it. "Excellent. I mean, we can talk about you hangin' at my house while my mom is away."

Cam couldn't take it anymore. "Bethie, what's up? For real. You've been giving off this weird manic vibe lately."

Beth had stopped dead in the doorway of the pizza place. She couldn't look at Cam. Embarrassed, she allowed Cam to drag her to a booth. The minute they sat down, she blurted it all out.

"You know, don't you?" her best friend forever said, looking miserable. "I knew I'd never be able to hide it from you."

And suddenly, Cam did know. This time, only a slight headache ushered in the vision, a rhythmic throbbing in her temples. Then she heard and *saw* Beth's mind.

In it was a picture of Emily . . . Emily swearing Beth to secrecy . . . about the birthday party.

Em was planning an at-home bash to end all bashes for the twins' sweet sixteen.

To keep the party a surprise, she and Dave would tell Cam and Alex that their birthday gift was going to be dinner at a snazzy Boston restaurant — with Beth invited along. The restaurant was famous for its lavish Halloween costume party.

Beth's job was to keep Cam and Alex away from home so that Emily would have a couple of days to whip Casa Barnes into party shape.

It was perfect. Beth's mom was going to be in Chicago that whole week, Cam heard her friend telling Emily. So Beth would "plead" and Emily would "reluctantly allow" the twins to keep her company, to stay with Beth after school and overnight for a few crucial days before their birthday.

Beth's job, besides providing a home away from home, was to keep Cam and Alex occupied. A shopping spree would work, Emily thought. Scouring Marble Bay for sumptuous costumes to wear to the dinner. Maybe a trip to the mall to pick out their own birthday gifts. A salon stopover to get their hair and makeup done for the bogus big night out. All charged to Emily's plastic.

Beth was to get them home Saturday night at eight o'clock sharp when the three of them, Beth, Cam, and

Alex, costumed to the max, would walk in on a radically stupendous surprise birthday bash — the details of which were blurry to Cam.

Candles burning. She could make those out. And little sparkling lights draped through tree branches. And . . . jack-o'-lanterns!

Jack-o'-lanterns?!

"Cami? Are you all right?" Beth was asking.

Are you *serious*? she wanted to shout. I can't believe they're doing it at home. Making it a Halloween party! As if she and Alex were going to have fun dunking for apples and carving pumpkins for their sweet sixteen. It was ridiculous, ludicrous, monstrous!

But Cam opened her eyes and nodded, though her head felt like a bobble-headed dashboard doll and every fiber of her being wanted to scream, *No!*

"S'nothing," she'd murmured to Beth instead. "Just lack of sleep. Alex and I have been cramming . . . for the PSATs. So, that would be a no," she said. "I mean, no, I didn't . . . I don't know what you think I'm supposed to know. I just felt like you were, you know, avoiding me."

She hadn't blown Beth's secret . . . when she might have so easily. All she would have had to do was say, "Yup, you're right, I know all about the surprise. Now here's what I want you to do about the party."

Instead, she'd opted to *trust* Beth and Emily. Which took all the *courage* she could muster.

Of course she'd filled Alex in the minute she got home from PITS. And she'd begged her sister to play along with the pitiful plan. "If I can grit my teeth and show for a trick-or-treat birthday debacle, you can, too," Cam summarized. "Dropping out now would amount to cruel and unusual punishment for Dave and Emily, who've been so —"

"Get a grip and spare me the gratitude lecture." Alex held up her hand like a traffic cop. "I know what I owe your folks. Besides, what else have I got to do this Saturday? I tapped into Cade's head a week ago and even *he's* in on the secret. He's gonna tell me there's an emergency, that he's gotta work late at the law office all weekend. Anyway," she added irritably, "it's not like there's a conflict. We haven't heard word one from the itty-bitty Initiation committee, have we? Talk about a debacle."

"Do you think it's all some whack test or joke?" Cam had finally dared to ask.

"If it is," Alex grumbled, "I can see how witches got a bad reputation."

The mall was crowded. And it was only Thursday evening.

Cam, Alex, and Beth were surprised to see hordes of costumed toddlers gripping plastic pumpkins filled with candy in one hand and their mothers' hands in the other.

Apparently, there was a Halloween party going on for children aged two to ten.

"I didn't know. I swear." Beth eyed the swarming Spider-Mans and Sponge Bobs, Harry Potters and Dora the Explorers with distress. "I didn't know they'd be doing Halloween early. I just thought we could check the place out. You said you wanted to get a new outfit for your birthday —"

"Maybe I should get a costume," Cam said, trying to keep the upset out of her voice.

"No prob," Alex assured Beth, digging into her jacket pocket for change to drop into the approaching kids' goody bags. "This place is loaded with inspiration —"

"Right," Cam grumbled. "I'll be Lilo and you can be Stitch."

"Um, Cam —" Alex had grown rigid. She was standing stock-still in the middle of the mobbed mall aisle. "Look over there." She signaled with her eyes. "That woman in costume —"

Cam followed her twin's gaze. "Ileana!" she gasped. "And Boris!"

A beautiful blond was wading toward them through

the Lilliputian throng. She was wearing a midnight-blue robe and carrying an orange cat.

"Ill what?" Beth asked, clueless.

Cam grabbed Alex's hand. Alex grabbed her moon charm. "It's either Ileana or another one of Uncle Thantos's clones —"

"Right," the gorgeous goddess sneered. "Like my fool of a father would really want two of me!"

"It's really you!" A broad smile broke across Alex's face.

They left Beth standing and staring and raced to their guardian witch. "What are you doing here?" Cam asked, stoked to see her.

"I thought Boris and I could score some easy candy," Ileana teased. "Are you ready for your Initiation?"

"You mean, right now?" Alex asked, taken aback.

"Not now exactly. Midnight will do," Ileana informed them. "You should be good to go"— she glanced at her watch —"in about five hours. That ought to be enough time for any last-minute arrangements."

"Like what?" Cam asked. "We've read every book you lent us. We've been practicing magick for weeks now. I've got a backpack full of herbs. So what do we have to do? I mean, are we supposed to change our clothes, grab a toothbrush, or what?" A hint of annoyance had crept into Cam's voice, the result, Alex thought, of weeks of hope and disappointment waiting for the Coventry call. "We don't need five hours. What's wrong with now?"

Ileana sighed. "Well, I thought I'd get in a little mainland shopping —"

"We're ready," Alex sided with her sister. "We've been hanging out all month, waiting to hear from you. Cam's right. We might as well go now."

"And what shall we do with your stunned friend?" Ileana asked.

Cam turned to see Beth coming toward them, smiling tentatively. "What are we going to tell her?" she asked Ileana.

"Sorry," their guardian said. "We're still in your Initiation month. I'm afraid I'm not allowed to help you."

"Alex." Cam turned to her sister. "What should we do? Will the Lethe spell work for —" Then it hit her. "Forty-eight hours?! But we can't leave now," Cam blurted. At Alex's questioning look, she added, "The Initiation, Als. It takes forty-eight hours. Do the math. We'll be gone on our birthday!"

"The party!" Alex got it. "Emily will crumble —"

"She'll be devastated, destroyed!" Cam turned to Ileana. "This is so not fair! My mainland mom has this secret extravaganza planned for us. We can't not show. She's been working on it for weeks, maybe months!"

For a moment, their guardian looked sympathetic, even sad. "I know," she said with a sigh. Then her features hardened. "I'm afraid it's entirely your choice. Like everything you've done or ever will do, your choices, judgments, and decisions will determine your worth and usefulness."

Cam looked at Alex, who shrugged. "I don't want to freak Em out, either. Honestly, Cami, I . . . I actually like her. And Dave. And then there's Dylan — he's like my best Marble Bay bud. He's like . . . a real brother —"

"But?" Cam's panic turned to impatience.

"But I don't know what's right. I don't know what to do," Alex admitted. "I mean, we can't be in two places at the same time —"

"Not unless Amaryllis shows up again," Cam snorted sarcastically. Then, suddenly, she brightened. "Als, if we leave now, get to Coventry early, maybe we can leave early. I mean, it's not even seven o'clock. If we can get back by seven on Saturday, we're golden!"

"Hi." Suddenly Beth was beside them, extending her hand to Ileana. "I'm Beth Fish, a friend of theirs."

"A pleasure to meet you." Ileana took Beth's hand in both of hers. "I'm Ileana, Cam and Alex's guardian witch."

Alex couldn't believe her ears. Cam gasped.

"Just kidding," Ileana said. "I'm a friend of the family."

"Right." Beth grinned. "I knew I'd seen you before —"

Of course, Cam thought. Ileana's main squeeze was Brice Stanley, movie star and secret warlock. Their guardian had been photographed more than once with the Hollywood hunk. But Beth hadn't made the connection.

"Oh, that's what you're supposed to be. A witch. Neat costume." The explanation had satisfied Beth. While she grilled Ileana about where she'd gotten her guardian witch outfit and such cool sandals and did the cat come with the costume, Alex and Cam tackled their issue.

And came to the same conclusion at the same time — Amaryllis.

It'll work, Alex silently decreed.

It has to, Cam noted.

We just have to find a spell to get her here.

The Traveler, Cam reminded her twin.

It's worth a try, Alex decided.

Oh, no. She's a witch! Cam's shoulders drooped. *She won't be allowed to help us.*

Alex slumped just as Cam had. Then she perked up again like a plant dosed with Miracle-Gro. *She's not exactly a witch. Not totally. She hasn't been initiated yet. She said so herself. She's still a fledgling!*

Does that matter? Cam asked.

Let's find out, her sister decreed.

"Excuse us for a minute." Cam snatched her twin's hand. "We'll be right back."

"Bathroom break," Alex said, flying after Cam.

"Why? Because you owe us!" Cam told the reluctant girl who was glaring at her with steely gray eyes.

"And anyway, you don't want to be on the island when we arrive," Alex pointed out. "Because that's when Lord Thantos will know you lied to him."

The spell had worked. Amaryllis, flustered and sputtering, had materialized in the dead-end corridor behind the rest rooms. Except for her pale yellow robe, their uncle's lackey still looked like Alex — and then Cam. Still under the original spell, she kept changing back and forth between the two girls.

The Coventry fledgling was trapped. And she knew it. Which didn't make her any less angry. "You're both going to be gone! How am I supposed to be both of you at the same time?!"

"Good question," Alex admitted. The trio stood surrounded by cardboard cartons and seasonal display pieces. The mall was preparing for Thanksgiving. Branches of fake autumn leaves, two nearly life-size cutouts of Pilgrims, a cornucopia, and a Godzilla-sized turkey with fanned-out tail feathers hid the twins and Amaryllis from sight.

"You could . . . um, wear a mask?" Cam suggested

feebly. "It's a costume party," she reminded Alex, who was looking at her as if she had two heads.

"Hello. Excuse me," Alex imitated Cam. "Her face isn't the issue!"

"It was just a thought," Cam snapped back. "Which is more than you had to offer."

"Still at it, I see," Amaryllis observed snidely. "Do you two ever stop? I mean, you can hardly stand to be in the same room —"

Alex and Cam exchanged glances. "That'll work," Alex announced.

Cam agreed. "Okay, you be me," she told Amaryllis, "and if Beth or anyone else asks where Alex is, tell them she's ticked off at you and sulking in her room or whatever —"

"Then you can say you're going to get her. Disappear and come back as me," Alex instructed. "Think she can pull it off for two whole days?" she asked her sister.

"She's got to. What's our option?"

"Hello. Still here!" Amaryllis waved at them indignantly. "Of course I can pull it off. I got you two going, didn't I? Just remember, I only get to be in your skin for two more days," she warned them. "If you're not back by then, your pals, your 'rents, your entire world, will know you for what you are — witches."

* * *

Cam and Alex raced back to where they'd left Ileana and Beth. They were sitting on a bench together, Ileana looking kicked back and comfortable, Beth stroking Boris, who was curled up in her lap.

"Ready to roll?" their guardian asked, not stirring from her languid position.

Excuse me, could you be any less discreet? Cam telegraphed, glancing over at Beth. But her friend didn't look up, didn't pause in her rhythmic caressing of the purring orange cat.

Ileana followed Cam's gaze. "Her? Not to worry. Boris is on top of the situation."

Alex studied Beth. "You put a spell on her." She grinned at Ileana. "I thought you weren't allowed to help us."

"Do you see *me* helping you?" the laid-back witch asked.

It took them a minute. "Boris!" they guessed.

"He's a very talented little beast," Ileana affirmed, reaching over to rumple her pet's silky fur. "Where most cats produce only allergies, Boris reeks spells. Lethe, forgetfulness, is one of his favorites. Beth will remember meeting me, but she won't recall this conversation. Boris will keep your friend company until Thantos's fledgling arrives."

CHAPTER TEN
RETURN TO COVENTRY

Before their eyes were fully opened, Cam and Alex knew they were on Coventry Island. The air was crisp. They could hear waves splashing against the rocky shoreline. The scent of herbs from hundreds of lovingly tended gardens rode the breeze.

And there was another fragrance — a mingling of savory pine, sweet lavender, and spicy rosemary — that told them they were in the presence of their mother.

Miranda rushed to them, sweeping them together in her embrace — and startling them with an unexpected apology. "I'm not ready," she said. "I'm sorry. I didn't expect you this early."

When she released them they saw what she'd meant. They were standing in the great room of Luna Soleil. The once-majestic cottage where they'd been born had fallen into ruin during their mother's long absence. She'd been hidden away, hospitalized for more than a decade by their treacherous uncle. And for all that time, Miranda had grieved for her twin daughters, who, Thantos had convinced her, were dead.

But now . . . the skylight above them was repaired. The debris of broken glass, splintered boards, and crumbling walls had been cleaned up. Someone was restoring the house.

"I'd hoped to have at least two rooms ready for you," their mother said, clearly delighting in their surprise. "Do you mind sharing one for now?"

"It's amazing," Alex said, turning slowly to take in the changes.

"You did this?" Cam could scarcely believe her eyes.

"For you," Miranda told them. "After your Initiation, this will be your home."

The Traveler's spell had left them woozy. But their mother's words pierced through the haze.

"Do you mean we have to stay?" Cam blurted.

"We can't," Alex said decisively. "We've got to go back. Why didn't anyone tell us —"

"I . . . I can't answer your questions. You know that.

I'm not permitted," Miranda said with a sigh. "Only your Initiation Master can do that. Wait here. Rest. Explore the room I've readied for you. I'll tell Rhianna you're here."

"Right after Initiation, I am so out of here," Cam told Alex the minute their mother had gone. "And since everyone around here is always talking about 'choices,' no one can make me stay."

"Ditto," her twin said, walking slowly around the room, trying to remember how it had looked when they'd been there last. She hadn't even realized there was a fireplace. Moldy old furniture had been piled in front of it. Now there it was, with logs stacked on the grate, ready for a cozy fire this chilly Coventry night.

The mahogany divan was gone, as was the bent-willow cradle they'd discovered on their last visit to Luna Soleil. A large new sofa with feathery soft cushions had taken their place. And the dangerously decrepit floorboards had been restored and now sported bright, beautifully woven rugs.

The door to the cellar, to the underground cave, had been replaced, too, Alex saw as Cam joined her. They stared at it together. The old weathered door was gone and so were the two-by-fours that had nailed it shut after Cam and Alex's first hair-raising episode underground — with Sersee.

The first time they'd met the devious young witch

she'd been jealous of them. She'd especially had it in for Cam — who, without knowing he "belonged" to Sersee, had fallen for Shane. And had been dumb enough to believe, for a little while, that the treacherous warlock loved her, too.

And, of course, he'd led her into Sersee's trap.

"Ugh!" Cam shuddered. "I don't even want to think about Sersee."

"And Shane?"

"I guess." Ha, she guessed? Like Alex or practically anyone else on this mind-reading, no-secrets island couldn't have picked up the thought in a nano.

But Alex had moved on. "Let's check out our room."

They'd expected some haphazard, half-finished space, but their mother had created a warm, wonderful place for them. The walls were of palest lilac, as was the shimmering fabric now covering the old divan that had been moved from the great room. Clearly selected with loving care, the rest of the furniture was carved of Coventry cedar. Cam and Alex could smell the clean woodsy fragrance that still clung to it.

The bed they were to share that night was huge, covered with a plump comforter and piles of pillows. And draped over the foot of the bed was their baby quilt.

Alex had thought it was lost! Yet here it was again, found by Miranda.

Alex picked it up and breathed in the fragrance of the protective herbs that long ago their mother had sewn into each patchwork panel. Cam took an end of the quilt, too, and softly stroked her cheek with it.

Artemis, Apolla, I am with you always.

The tender voice of Aron, their murdered father, seemed to rise out of the little blanket just as it had the first time they'd touched it. And as before, they reached for the amulets he'd made for them and felt them grow warm.

They sat together on the bed for a moment, each holding a corner of the quilt, listening, waiting for more.

Finally, Cam stood up. And as she did, the saying she'd found in her father's childhood room at Crailmore came to her. *An' it harm none.* The words were so strong and clear that they might have been spoken aloud. She glanced at Alex and knew instantly that her sister hadn't heard the adage, that it was meant for Cam alone.

Alex sat staring into the fading light of the autumn day, which streamed through sheer lilac curtains. It was two hours earlier here than in Marble Bay, she realized. She was about to remind Cam of that when her sister stiffened abruptly and her eyes drifted shut.

"Cam, are you all right? Are you having a vision?" Alex asked, standing quickly.

"In the caves," Cam whispered, her closed eyes seeing what Alex couldn't. "Still here —"

"Who?" Alex asked, trying to pick up a sound, a movement nearby. Cam might have meant anyone or anything. The cave beneath Luna Soleil connected to dozens of other caverns that ran beneath the north end of the island to Crailmore, the estate where their dangerous uncle lived. They'd heard stories of witches and warlocks gone mad who hid in some of the caves and of ancestral spirits who haunted others.

"I will not!" Cam said, speaking to whoever she saw in her vision. "Not even for you! I will not stoop —"

Then Alex heard it. A door banging open. The swish of a robe across the floor. The slow stealthy scuff of sandals.

Cam's eyes flew open. "Sersee," she said at the same moment Alex called out the name. "She's here. She never left."

"Aren't you the clever ones?" The violet-eyed vixen planted herself in the bedroom doorway. She was slender again, no longer the bloated balloon Cam had turned her into. Leaning back, with her arms crossed and her lips set in a taunting smile, she glared at them. "Welcome home, T'Witches. Your house is my house." She laughed.

"Your house? You don't have a house, Sersee. You scuttle like an insect under the earth; your home is a hole in the ground, a dark, wet, creepy cave," Cam blurted angrily.

"She's baiting you," Alex warned her twin. "Don't bite." *Remember,* she added telepathically, *kindness, compassion, justice, and love!*

But the sight of the beautiful, cruel witch had called up a swarm of bitter memories for Cam. Sersee gloating as she cast the painful spell that turned Cam into a helpless hamster. Sersee desperate for their powerful uncle's attention, willing to do anything for Thantos's approval and acceptance. Sersee jealous, scheming, deadly . . .

Ignoring Cam's outburst, Sersee crooned, "Your mother, that poor insane soul —"

"She was not insane!" Cam interrupted fiercely. "She was brokenhearted. And your pal Thantos lied to her and fed that grief every chance he got!"

"I am so sorry." The black-haired girl fluttered her dark lashes innocently. "But really, Apolla, I'm only repeating what everyone on the island says: that Miranda lost it, went mental, was off her rocker, out of her tree —"

Alex grabbed Cam to keep her from leaping at the malicious witch.

"But just look at this place." Sersee spun out of the doorway into the great room. "I'd say she's making a marvelous recovery." She looked up at the ceiling, squinting purposefully. "Personally, I preferred the roof . . . airier, more open," she said, focusing hard on the glass skylight.

"Don't!" Cam hollered, realizing what Sersee was doing.

The skylight shattered. Glass rained down onto the polished floor and handsome new rugs. A shard gashed the sofa. Another lodged in a freshly painted wall.

"Whoops, my bad." Sersee laughed.

This time Alex couldn't hold her twin back. Cam pulled free, sending her sister sprawling. With the speed and strength of the star athlete she was, she ran at the heartless witch, tackling her hard.

Sersee went down. Cam leaned over the girl, her fist drawing back automatically.

"What will it be this time?" Sersee hissed, grinning up at her captor. "What spell will you abuse? What violence will you resort to? Honestly, Apolla, I'm eager — or should I say 'dying' — to know."

"Cam, stop! Don't you see what she's doing?" Alex scrambled to her feet. "She wants you to hurt her, to hate her — because your rage will damage *you*! She wants you to do something wrong and evil —"

"Of course I do," the prone witch hissed at Cam. "Don't you? Don't you want to hurt me? Go on, I dare you."

Alex tried to grab her sister's arm, to yank her away from Sersee.

"Stay out of it," Cam shouted, pulling free of her.

"She's right, you know," Sersee whispered with contempt. "Your anger and outrage *will* hurt you." Her eyes, intense, violet, squinting deliberately, zeroed in on Cam's.

Instantly, Cam's vision blurred. Though hot tears stung and scalded them, she couldn't close her eyes; she couldn't look away. "Stop it," she commanded, dizzy with pain.

"Or what?" Sersee challenged. "As long as I live, Apolla, I will be your enemy. I will never forget the filthy trick you and that vengeful fool Shane pulled on me. So just hurt me however you want — before I hurt you!"

Cam could feel her cocked fist straining to connect with Sersee's twisted smile. Blinded by boiling tears, it took every ounce of her willpower to hold back. "I will not!" she said, as she had in her vision. "Not even for you! I will not stoop —"

All at once a wave of icy regret washed over her. Not so long ago, she *had* hurt and humiliated the vicious witch squirming beneath her. She knew now that she didn't want to do it again. Ever.

An' it harm none, her father's words rang in her ears again. *Harm none,* she repeated to herself as Sersee's evil glare stung her eyes. *I will harm none.*

Slowly, the anger began to drain from her. Her fist unknotted. Her hand fell to her side. With effort, Cam managed to pull away from Sersee, breaking the hate-filled stare that had connected them.

131

"You can get up now," Cam said. "It's over."

"No!" Sersee shouted. "Never! You can't just walk away!"

"You're right. I can't." Cam reached out her hand to help the seething witch up. "Not until I apologize. I'm sorry, Sersee, that I hurt you. The spell Shane taught me was evil, but I'm the one who chose to use it. I hope you can forgive me."

"Wimp!" Sersee slapped Cam's hand aside.

Alex raced to her sister, grabbing and hugging her. "That was awesome. You did it," Alex exulted. "You won. She's nothing but one of Thantos's flunkies — like Amaryllis and Shane —"

Sersee had gotten up and was brushing debris from her purple robe. She looked up at the sound of Shane's name. "You're idiots. You know nothing," she said. "Shane Wright is not Lord Thantos's flunky. He's his sworn enemy. He was reared to destroy your uncle! And you're too dumb to know it!"

By the time their mother returned, followed by a huffing, puffing Rhianna, the house was in better shape. Although the skylight was still broken and the new sofa torn, Cam and Alex had used the Restorer spell to repair much of the damage Sersee had done.

The girl herself had slunk away after failing to taunt

Cam — and then Alex — to new anger and vengefulness. It became clear that only by getting them to sink low could Sersee hold her head high. So it was with her head bowed that the once-haughty witch left — and took what she knew about Shane and their uncle with her.

"Precisely what time did you girls arrive?" Rhianna asked, surveying the room, noting every trace of damage with knowing eyes.

"It was shortly before five," Miranda said.

"Your daughters are about to be initiated." Rhianna's gold-flecked brown eyes glinted a warning. From a pocket in her ample robe she pulled out a plumed pen and a notebook bound in gold. "They ought to be able to speak for themselves."

"Of course," their mother said, taking no offense. "Would anyone care for tea?"

"Essence of rose hips, if you please," Rhianna ordered. "No milk, no honey." As Miranda left the room, the buxom Elder turned to Cam and Alex again. "Five o'clock. Seven hours before you were due!" She licked the tip of the pen and began to write feverishly in her book.

"Um, it was around seven o'clock where we came from," Alex ventured.

"That's only five hours early," Cam pointed out.

"Five or seven — it doesn't matter. What does is that you've upset the order of things. And by the looks of it —" she gestured with her pen at what damage was left in the room — "your Initiation challenges have already begun."

She was talking, of course, about their encounter with Sersee. "That part wasn't our fault," Alex tried to explain.

"We were totally minding our own business when —" Cam began.

"Do you think I don't know what happened?!" Rhianna pulled herself up to her full imposing height. "Have you never heard of the Situator?" She was speaking of the spell that allowed her to see them, to clock their every move if she chose, in a purified crystal of rose quartz.

"Of course we have," Alex said, annoyance creeping into her tone.

Suddenly, there was a noisy ruffling behind Rhianna. Cam and Alex jumped back as the wiry-haired witch's wings unfurled menacingly. "Enough!" she decreed. "If you wish to be initiated, you are not to leave this house until first light tomorrow. Is that understood?"

The twins nodded mutely.

"Unless, of course, you wish to leave the island — in which case you are free to go whenever you like. I would suggest, however, that you wait the required forty-eight hours to complete your Initiation. It will be a memorable two days, I promise you. Tomorrow you'll stand before the Exalted Elders of the Unity Council, who will test your talent for magick. If your mother and guardian are right, that part of the ceremony should not be difficult for you. It will be 'a piece of pie,' as your guardian called it." Rhianna smiled, pleased that she'd remembered Ileana's colorful phrase.

"Cake," Alex corrected her.

"Your Ladyship," Cam added nervously.

Rhianna stared at them as if they had two heads — each.

"The expression," Alex tried again. "It's 'a piece of *cake*.'"

Rhianna cleared her throat and began making notes in her golden book again.

Was that really necessary? Cam telegraphed Alex. *Did you have to be so —*

Honest? Yeah, I think so.

If their Initiation Master had intercepted their telepathic squabbling, she gave no sign of it. "The second portion of your Initiation will focus on your relationships, on how you deal with others," she continued. "That is both more important and more difficult than tomorrow's challenges. So . . ." She closed her notebook with finality. "Everything clear thus far?"

"I don't mean to be rude or anything," Cam said

carefully, "but I do have a general question. Why exactly do we have to . . . I mean what's the good of —"

"What's in it for you?" Rhianna snapped. "Your powers will be honed, sharpened. They will grow stronger — particularly when you use them to right a wrong or to help another," she recited, as if reading from a rule book. "Errors of magick and judgment will be caught and corrected early — in a sympathetic setting and manner — rather than causing you, or those you wish to help, embarrassment and pain later on. You will graduate from fledgling to witch, making you eligible to pass on your knowledge and wisdom of the craft."

"Does that mean we won't have a guardian anymore?" Cam asked, troubled at the thought of losing Ileana's sometimes impatient but always loving guidance.

"Of course not," Rhianna replied. "Ileana is pledged to you for life. But after your Initiation, so is our entire community. Should your somewhat flighty guardian become unavailable for any reason, you'll be able to call upon any other Coventry witch or warlock for help; all will be sworn to come to your aid. And you, in turn, will be eligible to become guardians, to take fledgling witches or warlocks under your wings —"

"Speaking of wings," Alex ventured.

"Certainly not." Rhianna headed off the inquiry — which, Alex realized, she must have been asked a thousand times. "Your Initiation will not entitle you to wings! Only years of service and the greatest degree of proficiency in your craft will earn you even a feathery start!"

"Lady Rhianna, I don't know if our mother mentioned it —" Cam began cautiously.

"Questions, questions, questions!" Rhianna complained, before Cam had finished her sentence. She'd wanted to tell the plump witch about the party Emily was planning; she wanted to find out *exactly* how long their Initiation would take. Would it be forty-eight hours from midnight or would their early arrival be counted? But Rhianna had had enough. "Why is it Initiates, who are expected to respond to the questions of their Elders, are always so full of questions of their own?" Their Initiation Master pulled out a pocket watch. "Late! Late again!" she exclaimed, and promptly turned to go.

Alex looked at Cam. *What about Shane?* she silently asked her sister. Before Cam could reply, Alex called out, "Yo, wait up. We want to ask you something else."

"Your esteemed winged Ladyship," Cam said quickly as Rhianna spun toward them. "It's about Shane Wright —"

"No it's not," Alex declared. "It's about this 'destiny' stuff." She lowered her voice, fearing that their mother might hear her and be hurt. "What if we — or me, anyway — decide I don't want to head up the DuBaer family?"

"That is not what I wanted to ask," Cam grumbled.

As if to say, "Give me strength," Rhianna sighed deeply and turned back to them. "I can only answer one question at a time! First Artemis. No one can force the responsibility on you. Only remember it was your own grandfather and your devoted friend Lord Karsh who devised this plan —"

"Because of the Antayus curse," Alex said.

"Yes. Antayus warlocks were sworn to kill the patriarchs, the male leaders, of the DuBaer family. No female, no witch, has ever fallen prey to the curse."

"Okay, so Cam and I are supposed to be immune. But what if we don't want to live at Crailmore and —"

"Do you still not understand? You have a choice!" Rhianna shook her finger at them. "It is your *decision*. But remember, your decisions govern your actions; your actions guide your life —"

"Is it my turn now?" Cam broke in.

A frightening flurry of ruffled feathers greeted the interruption. "The Wright boy," Rhianna said.

Alex rolled her eyes. "The wrong boy," she muttered.

Cam pointedly ignored her. "Yes, Shane. He used to be one of Lord Thantos's fledglings —"

"Yes, yes. I'm familiar with the boy and his family. And I have pressing business elsewhere."

"But you're the only one who can answer our questions," Cam complained.

"If I so choose," Rhianna informed them. Then she sighed. "Surely you've read Lord Karsh's journal. You already know what he had to say about it."

"He didn't say anything about Shane," Cam said.

"Yes," Rhianna insisted, "he did! Have you not been listening to me?" She glanced at her pocket watch again. "That's it! I'm hungry as a bear and I've missed the early-bird dinner again! Is your family trying to see that I starve?"

Cam and Alex looked at each other, perplexed. By the time they turned back to Rhianna, their Initiation Master had retracted her impressive wings and marched out the door.

CHAPTER ELEVEN
THE DAY HAS COME

The tapping woke her.

Cam opened one eye and squinted into the light.

Behind the sheer lilac curtains, Shane Wright was drumming his fingers on the glass.

She rolled over, looking for Alex. The bedroom they'd shared was bright with sunshine, and her sister was gone.

With her back to the window, Cam closed her eyes — as if that would get rid of Shane, make him go away — because already her heart had begun to pound; her promise not to fall for it, for him, was slipping away, like the quicksand he'd once lured her into.

"Cam." He knew she was awake. "I heard you were

back. I mean, everyone knows you're here — for your Initiation. I just . . . I couldn't wait to see you. Turn around. Come on, open the window. Let me talk to you."

She fought the temptation to put her hands over her ears. Too lame. Too weak a move. She rolled over angrily. Pulling the comforter around her, she set her feet on the carpet. "If you want to talk to me, wait out front," she ordered him, then turned away and, trailing the comforter, shuffled into the bathroom. And slammed the door behind her.

Alex, where are you? Cam sent a telepathic message. *Help. I need you. Now!*

Minutes later, as she was rinsing toothpaste from her mouth, the bathroom door burst open and her sister charged in — wielding an iron fireplace poker.

Cam almost choked. "Ease up," she sputtered, after spewing the foaming herbal concoction into the sink. "I'm okay. I just wanted to talk to you about Shane."

"And the word *help* in your shout-out? That was what, just a hiccup?" Alex groused.

Cam turned off the tap. "He's here."

"I know. I caught a whiff of him: peppermint, cedar —"

"And cloves," Cam said, realizing that her sense of smell had seriously improved.

"And skunk, I was going to say," her sister declared.

Cam let it ride. "I just want you to . . . to be with me when I go out there to talk to him."

"Which you're going to do . . . why? After the disgusting, to say nothing of near deadly, way he treated you, treated us, actually," Alex reminded her. "Why bother? Or are you still jonesing for the boy?"

"So not! I just want to find out —" Cam stopped in midsentence. She looked away from Alex, then turned back, flushed, her cheeks burning. "Maybe," she said softly. "I'm not sure."

Alex was impressed. "That ought to move you up in the honesty sweepstakes," she teased.

"Which is not why I said it," her sister snapped defensively. "Als, don't you want to find out about him, about his relationship with Thantos? Don't you feel . . . don't you get a sense that there's something smarmy going on there?"

"Smarmy?" Alex replied. "Yo, let me think. There's Thantos, who's been trying to off one or both of us since we were born. And there's Shane, who lies like he breathes. And you want to know what — if there's something smarmy going on? Dude, if you check *Webster's* for the definition of *smarmy,* you'll see their faces. But what are we going to do — ask Shane to tell us all about it? The one thing we know for sure about the boy is: Shane and the truth? Not friends. Not even acquaintances. To say nothing of the fact that as a Coventry warlock, he's got the perfect out. He's not supposed to answer any of our questions."

"Out loud," Cam added pointedly. "But if we can pick his brain — come on, Als. We're getting good at lots of things we couldn't do before. I tapped into Amaryllis's head when she was trying to lock us out. If I could do it, it should be a piece of . . . pie," Cam teased, "for you. It's worth a try, isn't it?"

"Sure. And we've got all day to do it. Not. Did you forget, today's the day we get tested on Applied Magick —"

"Perfect," Cam said. "Let's apply some . . . to Shane."

He was waiting at the front gate. A sudden breeze stirred his glossy pale hair. It fell over his azure eyes. The warlock tossed his head to clear his vision — and saw Cam coming toward him. His face lit up with pleasure at the sight of her.

Don't be so sure. Gripping her moon charm, Alex was a few steps behind her sister. She, too, had caught the swift change in the boy's mood but was not as convinced as Cam that it was all about joy. *His thoughts are locked down tight,* she told her twin.

How can he be so bad and look so good? Cam mused.

Alex frowned with frustration but Shane grinned broadly. He'd heard Cam's thought, too, Alex realized.

He can read you, she warned her twin. *Grab your sun charm and use the peephole.*

Cam's cheeks reddened with embarrassment, but she couldn't stop smiling. Even as she slammed an imaginary door shut on her thoughts, her feelings were loud and clear. She was hopelessly happy to see him.

And the tall, strapping warlock who was staring intently at her knew it.

He'd have had to be blind not to, Alex thought. *Your sun charm!* she reminded her smitten twin again.

But Shane wasted no time getting his arms around Cam. He lifted her off her feet and twirled with her. "It feels so good to hold you again," he murmured. "What happened the last time you were here, Cam . . . happened at Crailmore — it couldn't have taken place anywhere else. I'd gotten free of Lord Thantos, but he lured me back. It was being there with him that made me do what I did. It's Crailmore. It's an evil place. You've got to stay away from there," he was saying, his eyes holding her as forcefully as his arms.

And Cam's eyes — her extraordinary gray eyes that could cut through walls, start fires, see the future — were glazing over. She couldn't tear them away from Shane's insistent stare.

He was casting a spell over her, Alex realized.

Cam . . . Apolla . . . Yo! she was practically shouting through the peephole in her mind.

Nothing.

Cam's hands were on Shane's powerful shoulders. Her sun charm dangled uselessly at her throat as he spun her around.

Her sister might be helpless, Alex thought, but she wasn't — and she wasn't going to just hang back and watch the scheming warlock play Cam one more time.

For starters, she could follow their plan, find out what was on the rude boy's mind. Which should be easy, since he hadn't even acknowledged her!

Alex closed her eyes and tried to zero in on Shane's thoughts. At first she saw nothing, only heard a crackle of static and disconnected, barely audible words that meant his thoughts were scrambled. Then in the darkness jumpy lines appeared, zigzagging wildly, as if the static had become visible.

She concentrated harder. Focused all her senses.

The jerking agitated lines filled suddenly with blinding colors. A molten river of red, violet, yellow streamed behind her eyelids. The colors were random words, escaped sounds, hidden thoughts. . . .

Alex clutched her charm so tightly that the edges of the amulet almost tore into her palm.

"At Crailmore, I'm powerless around your uncle," the dishonest warlock was telling Cam, making excuses for the last time he'd turned against her. "He commands and I obey."

But soon the tables will be turned. Destiny will be done.

Alex heard it — so plainly that at first she thought Shane had said it out loud.

Then he *was* speaking aloud again, telling Cam: "He's dangerous. Stay away from him. Now more than ever, stay away from Crailmore. Promise me."

For my ancestors must be avenged.

Alex's eyes opened. What was he thinking about?

Shane glanced at her questioningly, momentarily unsure.

"Put her down," Alex demanded. "We have to go. We've got things to do."

Does it matter so much to you? the smirking warlock silently challenged her. *He's done you nothing but harm.*

Who? Alex wondered.

"Put me down!" Cam suddenly said. Shane had broken eye contact with her, and she was coming out of her stupor. "I . . . I'm dizzy . . . I feel sick."

"No problem." The brash blond boy spun to face Cam again. "I'll take care of you," he promised.

Alex stepped between them and put an arm around Cam's shoulder. "Thanks, but no thanks," she told the treacherous warlock. "You've done way too much already."

They were due at the Unity Dome at noon. To face possibly the most important exam of their lives. And Cam was struggling back to consciousness while Alex was hung up on Shane's secret thoughts. They needed to snap out of it and get ready.

Two gowns had been laid across their bed. One was gold threaded through with vibrant pink-and-red highlights, the other was a shimmering blue-gray. There were hooded robes to match. And velvet slippers that reminded Cam of the ones their beloved Karsh had always worn.

"You pick first," Cam forced herself to say, though even with somewhat blurry eyesight, she'd already fallen for the glam gold gown.

"Like I care?" Alex rolled her eyes. "You choose. And don't let the fact that one is the color of moonlight and the other the gold of dawn influence you too much."

"How cool is that?" Cam laughed, realizing that her sister had nailed it. The sunny gown was meant for her; the one that shone like silver moonlight was Alex's.

Once they'd had a delicious bath in scented salts

and soothing herbs, then dressed, there were two more rituals they needed to perform before setting out for the Unity Dome.

One was to rid themselves of ill will. According to *Ceremonial Preparation and Purification Procedures,* this meant making and burning a list of those who'd caused them grief. Two was to do a purifying meditation.

Cam expected the first to take longer than the second, given the list of villains who'd messed with them. But like so much on the island, the opposite of what she'd expected happened.

Agreed, a posse, a pack, a plethora of bad guys had tried to do them in. To name a few: Thantos, their depraved uncle; the ever-devious Shane; toxic Sersee and her crew, the Furies; and, of course, Amaryllis; their idiot uncle Fredo and the freaks that were his spawn, Tsuris and Vey . . . But listing them and trashing the list per Coventry tradition took less than a couple of minutes.

It was the purifying ritual that took longer. And, in the end, felt more centering and soul-strengthening. They did it separately.

Cam chose the rose arbor at the entrance to Luna Soleil as her meditation place. The summer blooms were gone, but nuggets of bright red rose hips dangled from the tangled, thorny branches. Whether flowering or hardened for winter, the rose represented love, which was, Cam thought, what she wanted to think about.

She sat under the arbor, closed her eyes, and let her thoughts wander. They went to Shane. Cam fought the urge to banish his image and allowed herself to feel shame, frustration, longing. . . .

When she'd questioned Rhianna about him, the Initiation Master had said that they already had the answer. That it was in Karsh's journal.

Karsh.

Lord Karsh Antayus.

The old warlock's image came into her mind. As always, he was dressed in black. His odd vest, a doublet it was called, and his trousers and slippers were all of black velvet, sleek and soft. His papery brown scalp showed through his thinning nappy hair, and through the white ointment he'd worn to preserve his ancient skin.

The pale paste had terrified Cam the first time she saw it.

Ileana maintained that Karsh wore it like war paint. The combination of herbs and powders that went into the ointment fortified the old tracker's strength and courage.

Tears poured down Cam's cheeks. The sight of his

face didn't strike fear in her heart now but melted it. She was so glad to see him again.

"So the day has come," he said softly in his raspy voice.

Alex sat cross-legged in the center of a stand of evergreens behind Luna Soleil. The soft rug of pine needles under her, the sweet scent of earth and trees, even the autumn chill — she might have been back in Montana with her beloved adoptive "Moms."

Back, back when Sara was young and vibrant . . . before cancer ate away at her lungs. This was the image of her protector that came to Alex's mind. And spoke to her.

"So the day has come," Sara whispered.

CHAPTER TWELVE
THE TESTS

The usually bustling plaza was empty as the twins, flanked by Ileana and Miranda, hurried across its cobblestones to the Unity Dome. Outside the splendid building, a swarm of children waited to catch a glimpse of Cam and Alex.

Excitement crackled through the young crowd. Sighs and gulps, nervous laughter, and shouted greetings heralded their approach.

"Good luck!" "Apolla, Artemis, over here!" "How beautiful they are!" "Happy Initiation!"

Ileana strode through the mini mob with dignified determination, setting the pace. Miranda brought up the rear of the little procession. Bookended by the women,

Cam and Alex were trembling. Their hands, gripping each other's, were sweaty and their lips were parched.

As the tall doors to the imposing building swung open, a babble of voices assailed them. The round stadium was filled to overflowing. Sunlight pierced the glass dome, illuminating a colorful, fluttering, noisy hive of expectant witches and warlocks.

That fell silent as the quartet moved across the marble floor.

At the center of the arena, Lady Rhianna waited with her colleagues, Lady Fan and Lord Grivveniss. They sat behind a judges' bench so tall that Cam and Alex could see only the tops of the gold bowl and twin gold boxes in front of the trio, and the computer monitor that sat in front of Lady Rhianna. Lady Fan and Lord Grivveniss would each "grade" the twins with stones, then send their marks to Lady Rhianna via e-mail.

The island's other Exalted Elders occupied the first tier of the steep stadium. Before each of them was a laptop computer. Row after row behind the Elders was filled with robed witches and warlocks. Alex noticed Sersee and her crew high up, near the back of the auditorium. Every servant or fledgling she'd ever seen at Crailmore was there, too — except for Amaryllis. Thantos's servant was still in Marble Bay.

"Welcome, Apolla and Artemis DuBaer. It is rare that two fledglings share an Initiation day, rarer still that they are twins," Rhianna greeted them.

Cam gave her sister a slight nudge with her elbow — not out of nervousness, but because Alex was studying the crowd and not really listening to the easily annoyed old witch, who could fail them if she wanted to.

"Check out the family row," Alex whispered, elbowing her sister right back and nodding toward the row where Ileana and their mother were heading.

"Ugh! It's Fredo." Cam couldn't control her disgust. Their uncle, the very one who'd admitted to killing their father, was there. "How'd he break out of the Peninsula?"

The Peninsula was the closest thing to a prison on Coventry. Fredo was supposed to be locked up there.

"They probably did a forgiveness ceremony on him just for our Initiation," Alex ventured.

Cam looked blank.

"Didn't you read *Policies of the Peninsula*? Forget Fredo. Guess who's cutting?"

Thantos wasn't there.

"No loss." As Cam began to turn back to the Unity Council bench, her eyes caught sight of a couple with an empty seat between them. The man had intense blue eyes and long blond hair pulled back in a ponytail. The woman was attractive, too. Both of them were dressed in black velvet, and both seemed strangely stressed out. There was an aura of anger and eagerness about them.

Though Cam was sure she'd never seen him before, the man looked familiar to her. Trying not to move her lips, she hissed at Alex, "Who's that guy in the black vest like Karsh's? He looks like . . ." Cam tried to place him.

"Shane," they both said.

"Bet they're his parents," Alex ventured.

"Bet it's his seat they're saving," Cam said.

"Apolla!" They turned back to the bench to face an irritated Lady Fan. She was impatiently tossing a gleaming stone from one tiny hand to the other. "The verbal part of the Initiation test will now begin. I suggest you pay attention. For each correct response, you will receive one sacred stone, which I will collect in these boxes. There is, as tradition dictates, one for each of you." Before Cam could fully focus, the tiny witch hurled the first question at her. "Apolla. What purpose does healing play in our craft?"

Shaken by Lady Fan's abruptness, Cam was unprepared. "Healing?" she stalled. "Healing is . . . very important."

Disappointed and disapproving, the little witch shook her head. No stones went into the gold box marked *Apolla*.

"Artemis, can you enlighten us further?" the white-haired, even-tempered Lord Grivveniss, asked Alex.

She'd studied this. She knew this. But it was as if a timer were ticking loudly, drowning out the answer in her brain. Alex closed her eyes and tried to see rather than hear the answer. There was the page, the paragraph, from *Moral Principles of Magick,* that held the answer! "Every spell, all magick," she began to recite.

"Is properly used for healing!" Cam suddenly remembered, cutting her sister off.

The next question was a follow-up, delivered by Rhianna. "What part does forgiveness play in the act of healing?"

"Most, if not all, healing comes from forgiveness!" Cam blurted.

Lady Fan frowned but grudgingly dropped a stone into Cam's box.

Steaming, Alex stepped in front of her sister. "And forgiveness only exists in a commitment to love and service to others —" she practically shouted.

"By releasing anger and fear!" Cam called over her sister's shoulder.

"Excellent effort!" Lord Grivveniss cheered.

Click. Clack. Both Elders deposited stones into the girls' boxes. Rhianna, who had closed her eyes in exasperation, now opened them and called out to the front row: "On the definition of healing, have you finished viewing the fledglings?"

"We have." "Indeed." "Ready, your Ladyship," came the responses. The Elders struck a key on their laptops — *Send,* Cam figured — and Lady Rhianna checked her monitor. With a nod, she dipped into the bowl and removed a handful of stones. These she dropped quickly into the boxes.

Too quickly for Cam to figure out who got which stones and how many of each.

"Don't do that again," Alex warned her, under her breath.

"They asked me first," her sister retorted.

"Silence! Artemis, Apolla!" Lady Rhianna was glaring at them. When she had their attention, she turned to her colleague. "Grivveniss —"

"Yes, well, now then," the old man harrumphed. "Apolla. Describe the forgiveness procedure recommended in *Policies of the Peninsula.*"

Cam bit her lip. Had the aged warlock listened in and chosen his question just to trip her up?

"Paranoid much? The Elders gather around the prisoner and recite to him every good thing he's ever done," Alex told Cam, just loud enough for the front row to hear.

A smattering of applause was cut short by Rhianna. "Did you know the answer?" she asked Cam.

"No, guess not," Cam admitted miserably.

Rhianna shook her head. "Lady Iolande, I believe you have the next question."

"Describe a spell, or variation of a spell, best used to heal," the dignified old witch proposed, "and give an example of its use. Artemis, proceed."

"The Truth spell!" Alex answered quickly, hoping to avoid a repeat of Cam's hostile takeover.

And then she was stuck for an example!

The Truth spell?! Why had she picked that one? How could the Truth spell heal? When had they used it last, used it or some variation —

Amaryllis! Without naming the devious little imp as the one in need of healing, Alex described the spell and how it had forced a "rebellious young witch" to reveal her true self.

"In just what way was that healing?" Lady Fan inquired.

After a moment's thought — during which, thankfully, Cam didn't jump in — Alex described how sick, how stressed, how terrified *she'd* been, for nearly fourteen years, not knowing who or what she was, only knowing that she was *different*. This secret had made her as sullen and snappish as the witch in her example, she said. Until she shared it with someone — who just happened to be her sister. Telling the truth, realizing and acknowledging that they were witches and not alone, had removed major angst from their lives. It had really helped heal them. "You're only as sick as your secrets," she concluded, quoting Karsh.

A sympathetic murmur rolled through the auditorium. When Alex looked up, Lady Iolande was nodding with understanding, as were several others in the stands.

"And don't forget — the truth will set you free!" Suddenly Cam was back in the game, grabbing her share of the limelight.

But Alex was feeling generous. Truth be told — no pun intended — it was the first time she'd thought of the Truth spell as something that could be healing. The realization pleased her.

"Apolla, can you give us another example?" Iolande turned to Cam.

"The If-you've-got-a-lemon-make-lemonade spell!" Cam said eagerly. Laughter rang through the arena. "Also known as the Transposition or Reverse spell," she quickly amended. She described the necessary ingredients and recited the spell she'd used in the lunchroom at school, the one that had saved Nadine from Skeevy Stevie and, later, turned the bully into his victim's loving protector.

"Ha!" Alex broke in indignantly. "I did that last part!" She turned to Lady Iolande. "The part about getting them to fall in love —"

"Ah, love." Lord Grivveniss sighed and smiled. "Truly, what is more healing than love?"

The questions continued, and each and every answer pointed to the same thing: that healing was the witches' art. And that love and forgiveness were the most important tools for healing.

Before the Q&A gave way to demonstrations of magick, Cam and Alex had taken the lesson to heart.

By the fourth question — identify the botanical and common names, scents, and uses of five healing herbs — they'd stopped interrupting each other. By the sixth — which sacred stones did witches use during the plague and for what purposes? — they'd stopped their goading and gloating. By the tenth — create a variation on the Truth, Travel, or Transformation spell that can stop anger — each of them had genuinely begun to hope that the other would succeed.

Love and forgiveness were in the air. So much so that Lady Rhianna, who could read even their most locked-down thoughts, had to warn them twice to stop helping each other.

Minding their own business was especially hard when each of them was asked to demonstrate powers that came easily to the other. Alex was called upon to use her eyes to see what normal eyes could not, to penetrate solid objects by staring through them, to glare hard enough to cause fire. The first two tests so exhausted her that by the third she was grateful to raise even a wisp of smoke.

She didn't exactly shine. Not any more than Cam did at identifying sounds too distant to be heard, raising and moving objects by focusing intently on them, and recognizing subtle scents.

Worn out and a little discouraged, they were surprised and revived by energetic applause and shouts of support and congratulations from the gathered crowd, who obviously thought more of their efforts than they themselves did.

Rhianna cut short their moment in the sun.

"Your next and most important task of the day," she announced, as everyone grew suddenly and solemnly still, "is to think of a person who, in your mind, deserves *no* forgiveness. While there are many through the ages who have perpetrated monstrous crimes, you are to think of those nearer to you. You are each to chose only one."

One what? Alex silently asked her sister. *One person who's so bad that they don't deserve kindness, compassion, justice, or love?*

Cam shrugged. *Pretty hypocritical, if you ask me. Who would you choose?*

Right off the bat? No contest. Uncle T, Alex quickly decided. *You?*

Cam hesitated, then sighed. *Shane, I guess.*

"They will do," Rhianna announced decisively, before either of them had said anything aloud.

Cam's cheeks burned as she remembered that there were few secret thoughts here in Witch Central. She glanced up at the couple who looked like Shane's parents. The seat between them was still vacant.

"Your final task of the day is to be of service to them," Rhianna said.

"You're kidding," Alex blurted.

Their Initiation Master closed her eyes as if she were hoping when she opened them again the DuBaer fledglings would be gone.

The crowd began to exit. Lady Rhianna took Ileana and Miranda aside. Cam and Alex stood in the center of the grand arena, not sure what was expected of them. Were they to stay or go? Find a way to be of service to their enemies here and now or take the task with them as homework?

All at once, Alex felt dizzy. Her heart and head began to pound; she couldn't keep her eyes open. By now, she recognized the warning signs. She was about to have a vision, she realized, reaching out to steady herself.

Cam, Alex called, not sure if she'd thought it or said it aloud, only that her voice echoed distantly. Her hand touched her sister's shoulder, which felt electrically charged yet stiff and cold at the same time. Cam, too, Alex realized, was in vision mode.

Suddenly, in the painful, pulsing darkness, Alex saw a swirling cascade of books. The final one, bound in leather so old it was dried and flaking, was called *Forgiveness or Vengeance.*

It was not a real book, she understood, as the cover fell open. It was a hollowed-out box meant to look like a book. Tucked carefully inside it was a sheaf of pages filled with the shaky scrawl of someone very sick or very old.

Karsh!

All at once Alex knew that her adored old friend Lord Karsh Antayus had written and then hidden away the manuscript. She and Cam had read it! It was his final legacy to them.

The unbound pages flew out of their hiding place. They circled Alex's aching head as if they were caught in a tornado. A single page sailed down slowly, landing before her eyes. The sentence that came into focus was:

In every generation, an Antayus will cause the death of a DuBaer son . . .

The Antayus curse!

Alex's eyes flew open.

Thantos! He was the son who had taken control of the DuBaer family. He was the one in harm's way.

Aron, her father and Cam's, had died at the hands of his own brother, not by a descendant of Abigail Antayus. The curse had not killed their father, Fredo had.

And Fredo? He was pathetic and powerless now. He'd been kept in the Peninsula and would be returned there tonight.

Only Thantos, so like his ancestor the treacherous Jacob, was likely to fall victim to the curse, to be stricken down by someone of the Antayus bloodline.

"Shane!" Cam called out. She was holding her head, trying to keep her eyes open, coming back to consciousness. "He's an Antayus. He and his father were both wearing the same kind of vests Karsh always wore."

"Shane A. Wright!" Alex remembered Amaryllis calling him that. "That's what it stands for — A for Antayus?"

Cam nodded and winced with pain. "That's what Amaryllis and Sersee were hinting about. His family must be direct descendants of Abigail Antayus. That's why Shane kept trying to win Thantos's trust. To get next to him. To carry out the curse. Als, Shane's going to try to kill Thantos."

"If he hasn't already." Alex exclaimed. "He's probably at Crailmore right now —"

"That's why neither one of them showed for the Initiation," Cam realized.

"And why Shane stopped by this morning. He tried to

cast a spell on you, to keep you away from Crailmore —"
Alex remembered the way the sinister boy had looked at
her, too. Realizing that she'd broken into his thoughts,
he'd smirked and silently asked, *Does it matter so much
to you? He's done you nothing but harm.*

Of course! It was Thantos he'd meant.

Alex grabbed Cam's hand and started out of the
dome. They had to get to Crailmore now.

"No. Wait." Cam wouldn't budge.

Alex panicked. Had Shane succeeded? Was her sister under his spell, fearful and forbidden to go near the
fortress?

"No way!" Cam insisted. "Hang on to your moon
charm. The Traveler's spell will get us there faster."

It was always colder on the barren north end of the
island. Trees grew twisted by relentless winds. Waves bat-
tered the high cliff walls, churning up sprays of icy water.

A numbing chill hit Alex and Cam as they emerged
from the spell to see Crailmore before them, standing tall
and foreboding on the barren cliffs.

One of the tall iron gates guarding the mansion had
been left open. It swung and creaked violently in the
wind. Shivering, they raced through it, still clutching
their amulets.

Their mother had left Crailmore only weeks before, yet the bountiful herb garden she'd created was destroyed. Whether by human or natural forces, it was hard to tell. The once-lush plot looked like an abandoned battlefield. Row upon row of plants lay slashed, shredded, tattered, as if a giant sword had cut them down. There were fresh footprints in the mud between the lines of demolished herbs that led to the entrance of the house. The massive front door was open. The mucky tracks went through it and down the long entry hall. At the end of the hall, in front of the paneled doors of the library, the tracks ended — and a pair of mud-caked boots had been left.

There was no doubt about it, the boots were Shanc's. The same ones he'd worn that morning, with his Antayus vest. Had he taken them off to sneak up on Thantos? Had he succeeded in surprising and possibly overtaking their wary uncle? Cautiously, Alex pushed the doors open.

The library was a shambles. There were books everywhere — books and pieces of books, torn pages, ripped covers, books sliced in two. Some of the shelves had fallen, some were broken, resting at odd angles in the bookcases. Thantos's desk was overturned. And the portrait of Jacob DuBaer had been slashed.

Alex and Cam hurried through the room into the

back passage that circled the first floor. They stopped at the stone stairway behind the kitchen. "Upstairs?" Alex asked.

"They could be below," Cam said, "in the caves."

The clang of steel on stone guided them. Following the sound, they raced toward the back of the house to the huge, stone-walled, old kitchen. A scorched stench hit them before they ran through the door. The odor of smoldering wood. And burnt hair, Alex's keen sense of smell told her, an instant before they entered.

Flaming logs from the immense fireplace had been flung everywhere. Having missed their intended target, Cam guessed, they'd left sooty scars across the floor and walls.

By the looks of it, Shane and Thantos had been at it for hours.

Deep gashes splintered the furniture, as if a giant cleaver had chopped at the chairs and work surfaces. The long wooden table, half a foot thick, that ran nearly the length of the room, was a collapsed wreck.

Behind it stood Shane Antayus Wright. His back was toward them as he bent forward, trying to catch his breath. The hilt of an enormous sword was wedged under his arm like a crutch. His black vest was torn just over his heart. Blood stained the knee of one trouser leg. The ends of his blond mane were scorched and blackened;

sweat drenched what was left of his long hair. Coils of it stuck to his brow. The smell of smoke drifted off him. When he lifted his head, they saw that his face was smudged with ash.

Shane squinted. His deep blue eyes strained to focus — on Thantos DuBaer.

The great bull of a man was on his back. His head rested on the fireplace hearth. His chest heaved as he gulped for air. There was a bloody slash along his cheek. He tested the cut gingerly with a gloved hand.

Shane's hands were raw and bare as he struggled to lift the sword. Once it was in his grasp, he started toward Thantos. The once-mighty tracker lay on the floor, unarmed, but still sneering confidently.

"Go on, grin," Shane gasped. "It will be your last. This is the sacred sword that has slain generations of DuBaers."

He heaved the weapon above his head and brought it down with all his might. But Thantos rolled, scrabbled, and skittered out of the way. The sword clanged as it hit the stone floor.

Thantos tumbled back to the fireplace. With his protectively gloved hands, he plucked a burning log from the hearth and hurled it at the boy.

Cam and Alex had been standing in the doorway, riveted, immobilized by shock. Too busy trying to kill each other, neither warlock had noticed them. But as the blazing log flew toward Shane, Cam sprang into action.

She focused her fiery eyes on the flaming missile — incinerating it before it reached its target. The burning wood became crumbling charcoal. Inches from Shane's head, the charcoal turned to harmless ash and drifted to the ground.

Stunned, both Thantos and Shane now turned to see the twins.

"Are you mad?!" their uncle bellowed. "This loathsome warlock is your enemy as well as mine!"

The moment the tracker's attention was off him, Shane swooped down and retrieved the sword. His eyes held Cam's for only a moment. "He's lying. I have no quarrel with you. Stand back —" he urged, turning to face his outraged enemy again.

"Stop him," Thantos ordered, his back against the fireplace bricks. "If he succeeds, your legacy, all that I've built and safeguarded for you, will be gone — Crailmore, the family fortune, the respect of all —"

Cam could hardly look at Shane. His wounds made her ache as if they were her own. She turned away quickly. "Respect?" she said to her uncle. "You're feared, not respected."

He waved his arm, dismissing what she'd said. "Fear brings respect. Haven't you learned that yet? People cower before you, beg to do your will. Fear, rage, resentment, envy — when your enemy is filled with these bitter emotions, he becomes weak! Weak as your pathetic friend here. I pass along to you the honor of destroying him."

Shane's cold blue eyes never left Thantos's face, but what he said was meant for Cam and Alex. "You can't destroy me. You can't stop me. Death is his fate; killing him is my destiny." He swung the heavy sword over his head again. "This meeting was scheduled four hundred years ago!"

"This meeting is canceled," Alex announced. She glared at the sword, willing it to fly from Shane's hands. But the moment it began to wobble in his grasp, he tightened his grip on it and turned on her.

The sword was shaking too wildly to be directed at anything or anyone. But Shane's eyes were steady, dark, and focused on Alex. He was trying to cast a spell on her, Cam realized. His lips moved slightly, stealthily, as he began the incantation.

"Watch out!" she warned, stepping in front of her sister.

A cyclone of snow suddenly enveloped her. Had it swirled around Alex, as it was meant to do, the icy funnel would have acted as a thick white veil, breaking her eye contact with the sword.

But heat was Cam's specialty. She beamed her

powerful eyes in Shane's direction, hoping she remembered precisely where his hands gripped the vibrating sword.

The whirlwind of snow melted. Cam's aim had been true. The hilt of Shane's sword had turned white hot. With a howl of pain, the wounded warlock released it.

At the same moment, Alex's telekinetic effort succeeded. Instead of falling to the floor, Shane's sword somersaulted through the air, landing on the broken table.

Not on, exactly. *In* was more like it.

The sword plunged into the thick tabletop — where, wedged deeply in the wood, it vibrated uselessly.

"Excellent!" their uncle exclaimed from the debris-strewn floor. Without getting up, he applauded them slowly and steadily. "I didn't think you had it in you to be so brilliantly ruthless!"

Opening and closing his hands, testing them to see if they were all right, Shane looked at Cam again, his eyes wide with shock. "I thought you loved me," he said. "I read it in your eyes, your heart, your thoughts —"

"She does," Thantos taunted, rising menacingly to his feet. "But they're fresh from the first day of their Initiation. They've been brainwashed by the Council. Now they love everyone, don't you?" he asked his nieces mockingly.

"We're pledged to help you, not to love you," Alex

said, not up for her uncle's games. "I'd say keeping you from being killed qualifies. As far as I'm concerned, mission accomplished."

"And you?" Shane asked Cam, moving swiftly to the table where his sword was stuck. "Are you pledged to help him, too?"

"No," Cam shot back, "I'm supposed to help you —"

"Which she's already done!" Alex told him. "She just kept you from making the mistake of your life —"

"Destroying the head of the DuBaer dynasty is no mistake!" Shane ranted, trying to loosen the sword. "It's my duty, my responsibility —"

Thantos's face lit up with cruel inspiration. "If your duty is to destroy the head of my family, you *have* made a mistake," he told Shane with malicious glee. "I'm not the one you want. It's them — my clever little nieces will soon rule the DuBaer dynasty. They, not I, are the rightful targets of your vengeance!"

"How stupid do you think I am?" Shane said, continuing to push and pull at the sword. "No witch, no woman, has ever led your treacherous tribe."

"Ask them!" Thantos laughed. "They have to tell you the truth. Honesty is one of the virtues they're being viewed on."

"Don't you ever get tired of trickery, Thantos? I'm tired of it, tired of you and your deceit."

Shane didn't bother to look at the burly, bearded tracker. All his energy was concentrated on getting the sword out of the table. It was giving way, an inch at a time.

"It's true, Shane," Cam said.

Alex tugged at her hand. "Only if we want it to be," she corrected her sister. "No one can force us to do it."

"Tired of my trickery?" Thantos said. Shane had ignored the scheming tracker a moment too long. "Then rest!" Thantos shouted, tossing a handful of herbs at the boy. "Only try not to breathe. My private blend is quite capable of withering your lungs. Oh." The hulking warlock pretended to have just thought of it. "But you must breathe . . . to live."

Alex recognized the mingled scents of a toxic combination: foxglove, mandrake root, valerian and . . . and something else.

"Nightshade," Cam ventured, recognizing the smell from the *Interactive Coventry Compendium of Scents and Nonsense.*

"I forget how gifted you are." Their evil uncle grinned malevolently. "Yes, some merely poisonous to the touch, others deadly when inhaled. Together, Shane, they should take care of your weariness and give you the rest you crave — permanently."

Without thinking twice, Alex focused in on the green fragments that had landed on Shane. One by one at first and then in clumps they began to lift off him, drifting off his lips and soot-smeared cheeks and torn vest. They hovered in the air in front of the startled boy — until Cam applied the heat to burn them up.

While Thantos glared at his nieces, Shane coughed and spat, trying to rid himself of any particles of the herbs he might have inhaled. When he was sure he was safe, he turned toward Cam and Alex again.

To thank them, Cam thought.

Wrong, Alex telegraphed her sister. *I thought you were premonition girl.*

For a moment, the boy they'd rescued from death studied them through cold blue eyes. "If it's true that you will rule, then your uncle is right," he said at last. "You, not he, are now my prey." With a final effort, he drew out the sword. "I will fulfill my vow. Abigail Antayus will be avenged."

"I could have told you this would happen," Thantos said. He had stepped back. He was leaning against the fireplace again, this time as a delighted spectator stroking his mangled beard. "Be my guest," he told the agitated boy.

Shane hoisted the heavy sword once more.

Alex rolled her eyes. "Slow learner," she told Cam.

Cam replied with a shrug and a quote from their high school English class: "'Those who forget are doomed to repeat.'" The twins' casual tones belied their sudden fear. Would they really be able to stop Shane?

Clutching their hammered-gold charms, they again turned their talented eyes on Shane and the sword.

Alex concentrated on the weapon, literally bending it to her will. She could do this. She *had* to do this.

Cam focused her laser glare on the two-timing — make that four-timing, she thought — boy's hands. Narrowing her metallic-gray eyes, she sent another searing jolt of heat to his fist.

Stubbornly, stupidly, Shane clung to the sword. His face turned bloodred. The sweat that had pasted his scorched hair to his skull increased. It rained down his straining face, soaking his shirt and torn vest.

Even as wisps of smoke curled from his hands, he kept trying to bring the sword down on them. Caught in Alex's gaze, the weapon was slowly turning back on itself. It looked more like a scythe than a sword now. Its shape, fittingly as far as Alex was concerned, was reminiscent of a curved quarter moon.

"Shane," Cam said quietly and calmly. "The battle is over. Thantos is not the true leader of the DuBaer family —"

"And, if I read Karsh's journal right," Alex explained,

"it was only the male leaders that Antayus sons were sworn to kill."

"So, whoops, your bad," Cam added. "Killing us won't fulfill anything."

Alex brightened. "Whereas *our* saving your miserable carcasses *does*." She turned toward Cam, gesturing for them to leave the baddies behind.

"You're right! We did it!" Cam exulted. "We helped those who deserved no forgiveness."

"Now don't forget," Alex looked back and shook her finger at Thantos and Shane, who both wore identical expressions of disbelief. "It's not nice to bite the hand that freed you!"

CHAPTER THIRTEEN
THE RECKONING

"Well, well," Rhianna greeted them as they arrived at the Unity Dome on Saturday morning. She motioned them forward. "Do you have any idea what you did?"

Yesterday, a line like that coming from the feisty Elder would have set off a stress attack. Today, the hard-to-please old witch was wearing a hundred-watt smile.

"We did what we were supposed to do?" Alex guessed.

She glanced over her shoulder at Ileana, who'd been trying to hide a grin all morning. As opposed to Miranda, who sat beside their guardian, inexplicably teary and honking into her handkerchief.

Neither woman had explained her over-the-top emotions that morning. And Alex and Cam had learned not to ask.

The crowd that ranged around the stadium was bigger than yesterday by two. Thantos, his cheek scarred, now sat in the family section. And between the couple who were obviously his parents was Shane, his burnt hair neatly trimmed.

The buff blond boy looked glum compared to his parents. They, too, had caught happy fever. They were watching the twins with expressions of glowing gratitude.

"And a great deal more!" Lord Grivveniss chimed in when they turned back to the Unity Council. The gangling old warlock also looked delighted — but then, he usually did.

Lady Fan leaned far over the judge's bench so that she could see and be seen by the twins. "You ended a blight on our community!" she announced.

"Well, good," Cam said. She and Alex looked at each other, mystified.

For the first time that morning, Rhianna displayed irritation. "Apolla and Artemis, don't you understand? A DuBaer, in this case two, saving the life of an Antayus, has broken the Antayus curse."

"Cool," Cam said, trying to be discreet as she glanced at her watch. "So . . . should we get started on today's stuff?"

"She's nervous about making it back in time. Emily, our . . . Marble Bay mother-type," Alex confided, "is throwing this 'surprise' sweet sixteen soiree for us —"

"Oh, yes. Happy birthday, Apolla and Artemis!" Grivveniss cried out enthusiastically.

Like tag-team disapprovers, Rhianna and Lady Fan each raised an eyebrow at him and shook their heads.

"She's been so good to me — to us," Cam said. "And she's so excited about this party, and —"

"Right," Lady Rhianna broke in. "Let's get started, then." She cleared her throat and changed her tone. "Are the Elders ready?" she called out commandingly. In the first row, heads nodded. Voices answered, "Of course," "Yes," "Certainly."

"Oh, you're going to like this, I think." Lord Grivveniss shivered with pleasure. "Nothing to do. Just stand here and listen."

One by one, the Exalted Elders came forward to address the twins. Each told of the good Alex and Cam had done, separately and together, on and off the island. The deeds went back to childhood, when a premonition of Cam's saved Beth's life, and Alex befriended Lucinda, who'd been a lonely outcast in grade school.

After the first dozen recitations, Alex was blushing furiously but, despite herself, was still eating it up. Cam became increasingly jittery and had to work hard to concentrate on what was being said instead of how long it was taking.

There were still several old-timers waiting their turns when Rhianna surprised everyone by calling a halt to the "Witnessing of the Good," as it was called.

"With your permission," she said to the twins, "we can proceed to the final activity."

Thrilled, Cam lost it. "You go, girl," she told the imposing witch.

Rhianna didn't blink. "In keeping with tradition, those witches and warlocks with whom you have come in contact during the Initiation period have also been viewed," she announced. "Their behavior and obedience to the rules have been evaluated. As have your own. Your last task is to complete your relationships with them."

Grivveniss was studying a long document. "The renegade witch Sersee . . . and, oh, Amaryllis, as well. I think we can consider them to have been fairly dealt with," he decided. "Shane Antayus." He turned to Rhianna. "I'd say they're more than finished with him."

Rhianna gave a curt nod.

"Fredo DuBaer . . . He's to return to the Peninsula," the still-smiling old man continued.

"Let's make short work of this," Lady Fan interrupted, snatching the list out of Lord Grivveniss's pale hands. "The only one left is Thantos DuBaer. He has been viewed and found in contempt of Coventry's creed and spirit. Let's see . . ." She studied the paper. "Turning against his nieces after they rescued him. Telling their mother that they were dead?!" The short old witch's eyes blazed. "That alone qualifies him. And there's more here . . . too much more. Taking away their birthright . . . Oh, yes, and the years he denied and neglected his only child, their guardian, Lady Ileana —"

"Goddess," Rhianna corrected her colleague. "She prefers that title."

"Goddess?! Never heard that one before." Grivveniss laughed merrily.

"If it was good enough for Lord Karsh, it is good enough for this council," Rhianna said firmly. "Lady Fan, you are right and wise. Far too much treachery has been visited on Apolla and Artemis DuBaer by their uncle. It is fitting now that they decide his fate."

Thantos jumped up. "How dare you?" he shouted. "I did what I did only to save this family. I alone held it together after their father's untimely death. I have managed their fortune and kept up their home. Have you any idea what it's cost me to take care of that drafty stone fortress? Or how much I paid, year after year, to keep their mother safe and well, to get her the care she desperately needed?"

"I wouldn't have needed it if you hadn't led me to believe that my children were dead!" Miranda stood suddenly and slapped her brother-in-law's face.

Thantos gasped and held his cheek. She had struck him where Shane's sword had left its mark yesterday.

"Enough," Lady Rhianna called. "Apolla and Artemis, you have been told that what you choose shows who you are. Your choices and actions define your character. You are now in the position of making a powerful and perilous decision. According to our laws and rules, you must decide what is to become of Lord Thantos DuBaer."

Still holding his stinging cheek, Thantos stood. "I've tried to protect you for years. If that meddlesome old warlock Karsh had not carried you away from Coventry the day you were born, I would have treated you as my own daughters!"

Cam and Alex glanced quickly at Ileana. Her father's lie was so outrageous that their guardian had burst out laughing.

"You *did* treat us like your own daughter," Alex said.

Cam finished her sister's thought. "You wanted us out of your way, too!"

"You were as scared of us as you were of Ileana!" Alex added.

Ileana's mother had been an Antayus. Fearing that his child might somehow trigger the Antayus curse, Thantos had abandoned his daughter when she was an infant.

"You *are* like her," the furious tracker muttered under his breath. "Ungrateful spawn, all of you."

Rhianna, who'd taken offense at Thantos calling her dear friend Karsh "meddlesome," had let the twins vent. Now, slamming her fist down, she called for silence. "Lord Thantos! You know the procedure. You are obliged to stand before the Initiates!"

After a moment's hesitation, a moment when it looked as if he was going to storm out of the dome, their uncle drew himself up to his fearsome full height and made his way across the row. Fredo, the brother he had used and abused for years, was the last family member he had to get by.

Alex heard "Have a good trip," followed by a high-pitched giggle. Cam spotted Fredo sticking his foot out. A split second later, Thantos stumbled and tumbled down the aisle, ending up sprawled at their feet.

Half the stadium gasped. The other half chuckled. Lady Rhianna's jaw rippled as she held back her own laughter. "You may stand, Lord Thantos," she announced.

As he got to his feet and dusted himself off with as

much dignity as he could muster, Lady Rhianna said, "Apolla and Artemis. The Council has viewed that you are wise. We have also found that your uncle Lord Thantos DuBaer owes you profound amends. Weigh your decision well. You must decide what to do with him — banishment or death or —"

"To banish me from my home, from Crailmore, from the land where my ancestors are buried, *is* death!" Thantos broke in theatrically.

Kinda over the top, Cam telegraphed Alex.

An Oscar-worthy rant, her sister granted. She'd had no problem reading the hulking tracker's mind. It was the fortune he'd stashed at Crailmore and in the haunted caves beneath the island that he was afraid of losing.

"Kill me — rather than send me away from Coventry forever!" he passionately declared.

Cam shook her head. *What a performance. Next to big bucks, the unc loves an audience.*

Especially one that cowers and cringes as it claps. The big guy feeds on fear and attention, Alex agreed. *Gotta have it twenty-four/seven —*

Now there's an idea! Cam said, stoked.

Rhianna cleared her throat. "I thought you girls had —"

"Elsewhere to be?" Cam blurted. "We do, your Ladyship. And I think we've got a plan. Right?" she asked Alex.

"Call it a compromise," Alex suggested. "We're definitely opposed to killing our uncle."

"Or letting anyone else do it," Cam said, trying not to look at Shane. "And Crailmore is so not our dream house. So —"

"Thantos can stay there. He can live here on Coventry —"

"But he's gonna be . . ." Cam looked at Alex, checking it out one last time. Alex nodded. "Ignored," Cam finished.

Thantos blinked at them, not getting it. "Ignored?"

Rhianna thought about it for a moment, then beamed. Lord Grivveniss looked around the arena to see if everyone understood. "They do," Lady Fan assured him. "All but Lord Thantos —"

Their uncle was laughing with relief. Arms outstretched, he turned to take in the crowd, circling the stadium for a victory lap.

As he approached, row after row, tier by tier, the witches and warlocks of Coventry stood and turned their backs on him.

By the time he reached the family row, the triumphant smile had slipped from his face. "Miranda," he pleaded, "you know I never meant you harm."

Without a word, Alex and Cam's mother stood and turned her back on him. And so did Fredo, chortling.

Last of all was Ileana, the daughter he'd deserted and disparaged. The child who'd never existed for him, who might just as well have been buried with her mother, who'd died at her birth.

"Ileana." Thantos swallowed hard, looked down, took a deep breath. Even now the words were hard for him to say. "I'm sorry." He spat it out quickly, shuddering afterward as if it had been a bitter pill he'd had to swallow. "I acknowledge you as my true daughter. From this day, I will love, cherish, and protect you."

Ileana had waited a lifetime to hear those words.

Alex and Cam held their breath as they watched her. They could feel their throats tighten, their eyes sting with waiting tears.

Ileana stood and turned her back.

There was no one left for him to plead with, except for Cam and Alex. He turned to them, his features distorted with anger and fear. "Apolla, Artemis. We are of the same noble blood —"

Cam and Alex gazed at him with pity — and then turned their backs.

When and how he left the Unity Dome, no one knew. But when Lady Rhianna cleared her throat, the twins turned back around and saw that Thantos DuBaer had gone.

*   *   *

"W-I-T-C-H!" Alex spelled it out. Her face half hidden by her silver hood, she was sitting at the edge of the ferry dock. Her robe was bunched up in her lap; her bare feet swung inches above the choppy waters of Lake Superior. "Do you get it?" she marveled, studying the parchment sheet Lady Rhianna had presented to her.

Gripping her rolled-up scroll, Cam was pacing, glancing impatiently at her watch. They were waiting for Ileana, because Alex had to have her steel-toed, lace-up boots before she'd leave for home. "Yes, I know. Very cool," Cam answered impatiently. "Wisdom. Intuition. Trust. Courage. Honesty. It spells *witch*. But I still don't see why you got more trust points than me. You're the most suspicious person I know. You don't trust anyone —"

"Maybe it's because *I* trust that you'll get to your birthday blowout on time, while *you* are having a meltdown over it," Alex noted. "Anyway, the Council gave you more stones in courage than I got — which is radically off. You're the total squeamish sista. But who cares?"

"I care," Cam snapped. "It took a lot of courage to unmask Amaryllis, resist Shane's spell, and wrestle with Sersee. But I can't believe we broke even on honesty. I mean, I totally stretched in that category —"

"But I aced intuition," Alex reminded her.

"And I got more points in wisdom," Cam shot back. "So we broke even. Big whoop."

"It is a big whoop," her sister insisted. "We made it, Cam-parison! We are the total witches. And today's our birthday —"

"Was," Cam said, "if we don't get going now!"

"Yo, leave," Alex grumbled. "It's your party, anyway."

Cam shot her a look. "You don't mean that," she said. "Just 'cause we're not being viewed anymore doesn't mean you get to be dishonest."

Holding Alex's grungy Doc Martens as far away as her slender arms would stretch, Ileana raced onto the dock. "Okay. Let's review," she said, tossing the boots to their eager owner. "You're both going back to Marble Bay. The Council has given you permission to stay on the mainland at least until you graduate, as long as you do there what you were born to do —"

"Help, heal, learn," Cam recited, trying to hurry things along.

"And we can return to Coventry whenever we want or need to. And every witch on the island is pledged to have our backs," Alex added.

"With some exceptions," Ileana said, "like my daddy dearest —"

"And others of his kind," Cam said, thinking of Shane and realizing that she was over him. Totally. For the first time since she'd met the sneaky, steamy warlock, her pulse hadn't quickened, her heart hadn't ached at the thought of him.

"Speaking of handsome rogues —" Clearly Ileana had intercepted Cam's thoughts. "I have elsewhere to be myself —"

"Date with Brice?" Cam asked.

"He's sulking with neglect," Ileana confirmed. With a wink and a wave, she hurried off.

Alex had pulled on her boots and had just finished lacing them, when a familiar icy breeze blew her hood back and sent her sister's gold robe billowing. The dock seemed to shudder suddenly.

"Still at it, I see." Amaryllis was back — toting three bulging shopping bags. She was her old self again, the spell having been magickally reversed at month's end. "Sorry." She shrugged at their stunned expressions. "I couldn't take any more."

"What couldn't you take?" Alex scrambled to her feet.

"Besides Beth's best sweater," Cam said, noting the familiar creamy cashmere the imp was wearing.

"You like?" Amaryllis did a modeling turn. "It's just a souvenir. Your pal's got so many. And she totally forced it on me when I did my I'm-Alex-with-nothing-to-wear shtick," the uninitiated witch bragged. "By the way, you —" she pointed at Alex. "You didn't show up for school on Friday. I couldn't be bothered running back and forth between classrooms all day. Anyhoo, I'm way spree-ed out. We did the mall, shopped till Beth dropped, pigged out at her pajama part-tay. Time so flew. And your forty-eight hours are almost up. In fact, you're on your way to Auntie Em's birthday bash right now — in costume, of course. Your bud insisted on getting in the Halloween mood."

Amaryllis studied their gold and silver getups. "I had you in black with blood-red capes. Oh, well, Beth won't notice the difference. I left her in a fog. Talk about surprise. Imagine how surprised she'll be when she arrives at your doorstep without you." The brazen imposter looked at her wristwatch — and Cam recognized the red Swatch Beth had gotten for her eleventh birthday. "Which she is about to do this very minute," Amaryllis informed them.

Alex sighed. "Okay. Let's do it. You grab the herbs. I'll do the Traveler —"

"Yesss!" Cam enthused. "Click your Doc Martens three times, T'Witch sistah, and recite after me: There's no place like home!"

CHAPTER FOURTEEN
A NIGHT TO REMEMBER

"Surprise!!"

Against all odds, it was.

Whatever they thought they "knew" about Emily's plans? Scratch that. No way were they prepared for the real thing. The gala maxed out on bombshells, shocks, hoots of joy, gasps of wide-eyed amazement — accompanied, later, by buckets of grateful tears.

The Traveler's spell had done its thing. One minute the twins were on the dock at Coventry, the next they were in front of Cam's house in Marble Bay. And Beth was between them, her sinewy arms linked in theirs.

From inside, sounds flew out at them, a glut of

psyched giggles and whispers. Sights circled their brains, a manic slide show of lights and faces. Before they could process any of it, the front door flew open and a party-sized pack of revelers chorused, "Surprise!"

Camera flashes momentarily blinded Alex, but Cam recognized a field of friends, as lit up as the jack-o'-lanterns that decoratively lined the walkway.

Shouts of "Happy Birthday!" and "Did you know? Were you surprised?" were answered by, "They must have, they're in costume!" "No way, look at their faces, they were stealthed, man, we did it!"

The shout-outs were punctuated with grateful laughter and relief: It was time to get the party started. Cam and Alex were whisked into the house and straight into a free-for-all hug-o-rama — glowing faces morphed into embraces, squeals, stoked smiles, and yelps of joy. Everyone talked at once, loudly, to be heard over the raucous music that kicked in on cue:

"They say it's your birthday!"

The Beatles. The "Birthday" song.

"It's my birthday, too, yeah!"

Which could have been written for twins.

The girls' minds were still half on Coventry and the amazing events of the last two days. But the party's energy was irresistible.

Snap: Alex got her first big mind-blow of the night. The party she'd been dreading? A new day had dawned, and with it an unexpected attitude adjustment: She was suddenly psyched. Totally there. All over it — mind, body, and soul.

It was as they'd known it would be, a Halloween-themed sweet sixteen. Everyone was in costume. Cam and Alex, draped in their Coventry robes, were technically not. But no one realized it.

And who was there? Hello, who wasn't? No matter how artful the face paint, how creative the getup, how killer the mask, no camo could conceal this crew. Cam didn't need her see-through lenses to know who was who. These were the friends, the family, the neighbors, even her soccer coach, the loved ones who'd mattered — way back when, in spite of it all, and for always.

Alex needed no mind-reading skills. The vibe popping off the crowd was electric — and their excitement and happiness and loving thoughts were for her, too. Every bit as much as they delighted in surprising and celebrating Camryn, these people, strangers to her only a summer ago, were including her equally and fully in their good wishes. Alex couldn't deny it, not after trying and failing to fend off the umpteenth rib-crushing hug.

The Six Pack had swooped down and surrounded the twins. And what a sight they were! Beth, whose frizzy hair was tucked under a lustrous blond wig, they realized now, was part of a trio of costumed heroines. Tall and rangy, she was Cameron Diaz to Kristen's dark-haired, chic Lucy Liu, and Amanda's over-the-top Drew Barrymore.

"Charlie's Angels!" Cam got it.

"Camryn's Angels," Beth gleefully corrected her.

"Cam and *Alex's* Angels," the ever-equal-op Amanda jumped in.

"What are *you*?" Alex quizzed Sukari. The plump, brainy, and usually reserved Suke was poured into a designer-worthy, gold-and-cocoa formfitting dress.

Grinning at their cluelessness, Sukari produced, from behind her back, a telling accessory: an imitation Academy Award. "Don't you know?" She paused. "I'm Halle! Halle Birth-berry!"

Alex cracked up and Cam threw her arms around the science-terrific Bond girl.

"Let me guess. You came as . . . twins!" An irrepressible grin took the edge off Brianna Waxman's attempt at cynical. The pint-sized diva was swaddled in shiny black spandex, from the cat's ears jutting from her highlighted hair to the towering stiletto heels of her thigh-high boots. "How Mary Kate and Ashley."

"Bree opted for a come-as-you-are costume. Right?" Kristen prompted her best bud.

"She thinks she's a pussycat?" Alex was flabbergasted at how far off base Bree's vision of herself was.

"Of course not," the spandexed girl said. "I'm . . . catty."

"Catty. Get it?" Amanda asked — unnecessarily, since everyone had broken up at Bree's answer.

"Actually, Daddy got me an exact dupe of Michelle Pfeiffer's *Batman* getup," Bree insisted, twirling her tail. "She and I are so the same size. And you're supposed to be?"

"Witches," Cam answered.

"Twin witches," Alex amended.

With a glance at her sister, Cam said, "We're T'Witches."

"Ooooh, that's so cute," Amanda cooed.

"But what? You ran out of money for the accessories?" Bree challenged. "Where are the brooms and pointy hats?"

Exchanging smiles, Cam and Alex shrugged. It was Dylan who unwittingly bailed them by breaking into the Six Pack circle and crowing, "That's old school. They're new-jack witches!"

"And look at you!" Cam whirled, pointing. Her little bro was all tricked out, not as the extreme sk8er boi they might have expected, but as a decidedly retro folkie. His hair was long and straggly, a stick-on, soul-patch goatee was on his chin and, tellingly, an acoustic guitar with a tie-dyed strap was draped over his shoulder. Dylan Barnes had gone Dylan, Bob.

Amid the hubbub and delighted squeals of confusion, Cam felt a warm hand on her shoulders. It instantly calmed and centered her. She knew at once who had touched her; the surprise was that her heart leaped.

"Hi, birthday babe," he was saying as she turned slowly, raising her chin to meet the warm, dark eyes of Jason Weissman. Tall and muscular, he'd come dressed as Jason Kidd, basketball star supreme — the tank top doing nice justice to his pecs, Cam noted.

"You . . . you . . . you're here," she stammered, then caught herself. Why wouldn't he be? In whatever way she wanted — friend, or boyfriend — Jason would always be here. Years ago, he'd decided to be her rock. And in some way, up front or indirectly, she'd accepted.

"Happy birthday, sweet sixteen," was all he said, before letting his arm slide to the small of her back, gently guiding her forward, where another batch of well-wishers waited to embrace her. There were more of Cam's school friends, soccer teammates, girls she'd befriended from rival teams. Soon, she and Alex were swallowed up in more hugs and kisses and "happy birthdays."

Alex was jazzed, witnessing the scene between her sister and Jason — Cam's "soul mate," was what she was thinking. She barely noticed when the boy who might be her own made his way through the sea of people to wash up at her elbow. It wasn't until he squeezed it that Alex jumped, startled. Okay, the costume — a French beret and silly painted-on mustache — was pure cheese-ola. Or maybe *fromage* was a better word. But Cade wasn't. Cheesy that is — not when he pulled off the mustache, gently pressed his lips to hers, and whispered, *"Bon anniversaire.* Happy birthday, *ma petite choucroute."*

Over her weak "thank you," he teased, "Alex, you're blushing," and let his fingertip trace her cheek. Alex grinned.

But something was missing.

Cam sensed it first and scanned the crush for her mom. Emily and Dave were not immediately among the throng of well-wishers. So where were the masterminds of this mega event? It took a moment, but she found them, pressed against the back wall of the front hall, holding hands, basking in the glow of a party about to go very, very right.

They were wearing matching black T-shirts on each of which was the legend EM.

Em and Em?

Eminem!

Cam got it!

When her eyes met theirs, the adoptive couple who were her parents in every way but biological, Cam saw the joy and love and felt a kind of click, an allegiance renewed.

The past one year-plus — ever since she and Alex had discovered each other — had strained the fabric of the Barneses' carefully woven family bonds. But it had not ripped them apart. As much as any witch or warlock on Coventry, this extraordinary couple had her back. Hers and Alex's.

All this Cam got in an instant. No words needed. Which was a good thing. Because she could not have trusted herself to speak. The lump in her throat would have made it impossible.

She felt Alex's arm slip around her waist, providing the strength she needed to move away from the partyers to make her way to Dave and Emily. The embrace was a four-way, and it would have been a mutual sob-fest, had Dylan not broken in, loudly so everyone would follow. "Dudes, let's move! Backyard, outside — or this party's gonna start without us!"

Cam's kid brother wasn't kidding. At their first glimpse of the backyard, Cam's left hand and Alex's right clasped over their mouths in perfect sync. The entire yard, from the weeping cherry tree that marked the far left corner of their property to the row of honeysuckle hedges that bordered the right, had been transformed into Party Central, circus style.

Ringmaster-mom Emily had used her skill as a decorator to full effect. She'd rented two huge party tents for her girls and had them customized.

Based on the twins' necklaces, the entryway to one tent was decorated with radiant sunbursts — substituting soccer balls for the blazing yellow suns in the center. Stenciled in glitter above the entrance were the words CAM'S SOCCER LEAGUE.

The tent next to it was sprinkled with silver stars and crescent moons and labeled ALEX'S HARD ROCK CAFÉ.

At any other time, Alex would have gone queasy over the too-cute décor. But this moment, her stomach fluttered for another reason. It was Cade on one side, Dylan on the other, practically pushing her inside the moon tent. Alex understood a minute too late: There were more custom surprises waiting inside, and not very patiently, for her.

"What took you so long, girlfriend?! Thought I'd grow old waitin'!"

Not even oversized freckles and a horn-honking fake red nose could disguise the familiar, round, open face greeting Alex. "Get in here so I can give you a birthday hug!" Lucinda Carmelson ordered. Her ear-to-ear grin was widened by an exaggerated, painted-on clown smile. Lucinda, the once and forever BFF, rushed Alex, grabbed her in a bear hug so tight, it nearly cut off her breathing.

"Yo, make room, I got dibs, too." The voice, like the boy himself, was warm and sweet as chocolate.

"Evan Fretts!" Alex, released from Luce's frenzied grip, was practically hyperventilating. Evan was here! If Lucinda owned best friend forever status, Evan was Alex's Montana main man: the boy who, despite his own plentiful problems, had always watched out for her.

He'd never been to Marble Bay before. Yet here he was, so very Evan — solid, still, standing his ground with open arms, hale and hottie as ever. But where were his dreadlocks? Was it for the party that he'd gone all Captain Peroxide? "You like?" Evan asked, running his fingers through the new 'do.

Alex tried to collect herself, but failed. "You guys! You flew here all the way from Crow Creek! How could you afford —" She knew the answer before finishing the sentence. They couldn't afford it. Emily and Dave had flown them in. Her legal guardians had known what was important to Alex, and how to translate that into the kind of party the girl who hated parties would be all over.

Lucinda was squealing, having spied Cade a second before a stream of Dylan-led guests flooded Alex's tent.

"Is this him? This must be him!" Snatching Alex's arm, she demanded, "Tell all! Now!"

Alex laughed. A good thing, 'cause no way was she crying, not in front of the slackers, boardies, and surfers who were crowding in.

Luce. Alex couldn't get over it. You could take the girl out of the wide-open spaces of Montana, but you could never take the wide open-heartedness, the smiling directness, out of the girl. And why would anyone want to? "Fill you in later," Alex promised as Dylan got the music cranking.

Music had been the insta-bond between him and Alex, their native language. So trust Dyl to know what kind of mix to master for Alexandra Fielding's sixteenth birthday. Nothing you could dance to, not a happy-go-hooky pop song in the bunch. Instead, it was a blend of alternative, brat rock, a pulse of punk, and okay, call it folk, the every-couplet-tells-a story kind of music. A sound track for Alex's life, for her heart.

All props went to Emily for the chow-down. She wandered into Alex's tent now and sidled up to her legal charge. She hadn't, she reported, actually *cooked* anything — they both laughed at that admission — but applied her creative streak to what should be served. Three buffet stations had been set up, all with unfussy, untrendy, finger food. Mini hot dogs, zucchini and mozzarella cheese sticks, corn on the cob, chicken wings, fries both curly and stringy, tacos, burritos . . .

Alex stopped surveying just then. At the end of the tables were . . . O.M.G. . . . framed family photos! *Her* family photos! Baby Alex and toddler Alex, down by Crow Creek, Sara hovering over her. And school pictures, too, one bad-hair class pic after another of a decidedly un-smiling little girl with huge gray eyes.

She caught sight of Luce, who winked, and Alex shook her head. *You shouldn't have,* she thought. When Evan laughed, she could have sworn he'd heard her thoughts.

There was one photograph at the end of the table that had not been lugged from Montana. It was of an old white-haired gent, cradling two babies in his arms, babies who — if you looked very, very closely — were wearing hammered-gold necklaces, one a crescent moon shape, the other a sun.

Alex knew not to ask Emily where that pic had come from. The good woman who'd worked so hard and so successfully to give Alex a wonderful sweet sixteen would not have known the truth. Which had to be: The photo had appeared courtesy of Ileana.

Was she here, too? Was that possible? The tent curtain was thrown open. But it wasn't her guardian witch. Instead, Amanda and Sukari wandered in and were immediately sidetracked by Lucinda and Evan, who introduced themselves. In a moment, an animated chat was going on. Others showed up. Friends from school, including the ex-bullies club of Eddie Robins and Skeevy Stevie, plus his "girl," Nadine, and more of Dylan's posse, the kids she most often ate lunch with. There were more, some she wasn't even sure she knew.

It's the free fun and food they've come for, she caught herself thinking — until another voice rang in her head. Cam's. *Just 'cause we're not being viewed anymore doesn't mean you get to be dishonest,* her sister had scolded on the dock. *Okay,* Alex had to admit. Maybe it wasn't *just* the freebies that had drawn this crowd. Maybe they were really here for her.

It didn't matter, though, did it? Whatever the reason, everyone seemed psyched and ready to party. And the happy excitement they brought with them was the real deal.

Released by Lucinda, Cade was behind her now, and his arms were around her. Alex leaned back into his chest, watching everything and everyone. She could not wipe the grin off her face.

* * *

In the tent next door, her identical twin wore an identical grin. The music, supplied by a neighbor doubling as DJ spinner-scratcher, was pulsing, loud, fast, and fun. And Cam was dancing, first with Jason, then with Jason and Beth, then with Jason, Beth, Brianna, and Kristen. So were the dozens of others, to music that mirrored the upbeat mood. Very Cami, very much, very all the way!

As she moved and swayed to the beat, Cam felt herself shedding the stress of the past. Had it been an entire month? She'd been smack in the middle of family feuds, curses, rescues, and revelations. She'd dealt with Amaryllis, and Sersee, and Shane again, this time seeing him for who and what he really was. She'd been bombarded with questions, challenges, urgent decisions, life-or-death choices, and finally, she'd been initiated. She'd become what everyone on Coventry believed she was born to be. . . .

Now that she was back, now that she was here, literally in her own backyard, secure in her very own spotlight, the surprise for her — yes, another one — was that she didn't feel as if she was in "another world." Her Coventry life was simply another part of her. A vital piece of the total Cam. And she was okay with that.

"Close your eyes and open wide." When so directed

by Brianna, the boss, one did exactly as ordered. Cam was rewarded with a spicy tuna roll: scrumptious! It was part of the buffet, the kind of smorgasbord she'd have ordered had she been in charge of this party. As if he'd read her mind, Dave winked and pretended to display empty pockets. "Your mom went all out," he joshed. "Only the best for our sunshine girl."

He was so not exaggerating. Cam and her buds had their pick of delicious exotic fare — from creamy pastas to succulent sushi, delicately wok-sautéed meats, mounds of shrimp, lobster claws and clams, baby vegetables and mesclun salads, melons and mousses and cream puffs . . . it went on and on!

At the end of the buffet table were the family photos. Which had the totally desired effect: Cam-barrassment! There was three-year-old Cami at the beach, sausaged into a frilly pink polka-dot bikini, complete with floppy sun hat, sturdy little thighs, and chunky fingers gripping a plastic pail and shovel. Six-year-old Cam proudly and toothlessly holding up the dollar bill the tooth fairy had left her. And did Emily have to include the absolute worst seventh-grade hair ever? What had possessed her to perm it, anyway? Oh, well, Cam laughed — it was all part of a surprise party. The pics were nothing if not giggle-inspiring.

"Where'd you get this one?" Dylan, who'd arrived to

check out her tent, pointed to a framed photo he'd never seen before. Quick as a flash, Dave was at his son's side to respond, "I found it in a thrift shop. The old guy looked like he was holding twins. I couldn't help picking it up."

Cam slipped her arm around her dad's waist and whispered in his ear, "I'm glad you did. I'll keep it forever."

Dave — were those tears in his eyes? — couldn't keep the words inside. "I hope you'll keep me forever, too. I mean . . . you'll always be . . . my little girl —"

His serious expression gave way to a helpless smile. "Go on, have fun," he directed, then turned and briskly exited the tent. Cam watched him go, sniffling back the quick itch of her own tears. She was doing as Dave had ordered when a sudden premonition, followed by an amazed shriek, sent her bolting outside.

The frenzied cry was Brianna's. "O.M.G. He did it!" she shrilled as Cam emerged into the candlelit twilight. Alex had rushed outside, too. "Daddy must have sent him!" Bree declared, wriggling with excitement.

Moving toward them was a trio of costumed guests — all of them in flowing velvet robes. The figure in the center was the one Bree had lost it over. Not even a plumed pirate hat and an eye patch could disguise Brice Stanley. In addition to more than twenty movies, his famous face had appeared on the covers of countless magazines under banners that read HUNK OF THE YEAR, OUR FAVORITE HOTTIE, and HOLLYWOOD'S STUDLIEST STAR.

Brianna's father had produced Brice Stanley's most recent movie — and at Bree's wheedling and whining insistence had invited the Six Pack to the premiere. Of course, the manic cat-girl would take credit for his showing up.

And just as well, Cam thought, as she recognized the women flanking Coventry's most successful warlock.

"It's your 'guardian witch.'" Beth, who'd followed Cam out of the tent, recognized Ileana from the mall. Brice's other companion had the same piercing gray eyes as the twins and, curling from under her burgundy hood, the same sunny auburn hair.

"Hi, Brice! Remember me? Eric Waxman's daughter —" Ignoring the women, Bree had managed to cut the actor out of the herd. With her scrawny arm locked in his, she began to shepherd Brice possessively through the awestruck crowd.

Ileana inserted herself between her cousins and former charges, who were now — according to Coventry law — her equals. "Happy birthday, T'Witches," she murmured. "I hope you don't mind our crashing. Two stellar occasions in the same day. We just couldn't stay away."

The commotion had attracted Dave and Emily. As Cam's adoptive mom turned questioningly toward her husband, the woman in the burgundy cape came toward them.

The beautiful stranger extended her hand. "I'm Miranda DuBaer, a friend of Mr. Stanley's. He and his date, my niece Ileana, asked me to come along. I hope you don't mind. I've been wanting to meet the two of you for a while now —"

Cam heard and gasped. Alex heard Miranda, too, and was surprised at how her stomach dropped with dread at even the possibility that their birth mom's presence might upset Dave and Emily. *But they don't know who she is,* Cam telegraphed her twin, although she was experiencing the exact same fear.

Which soared to queasy terror when Dave's mouth fell open, and Emily burst into sudden tears. They knew! One look at Miranda had told them who she was: Camryn and Alex's birth mother.

"Get over yourselves," Ileana hissed at the twins. "Have you learned nothing? Our lives are pledged to heal, not hurt."

"I'm so pleased to meet you," Miranda was saying to Dave and Emily. "You've reared two wonderful girls. Two very special children who desperately needed your love. Yours," she emphasized, holding their stunned gazes. "No one could have done it better. I came especially to assure you of that. And to thank you — with all my heart."

"Oh, no," Cam groaned.

"We've got to do something," Alex asserted.

"The Lethe spell," Cam remembered.

"Got herbs?"

"Valerian root," Cam said, reaching into the pocket of her robe as they hurried toward Emily and Dave. "And a smidge of rosemary for contentment and love."

"Hey, you guys." Alex went for bright and carefree. "We just wanted to say how incredibly flawless this bash is."

"Awesome," Cam agreed with all her heart. "I couldn't have planned it better myself."

"This is Miranda DuBaer," Dave said, glancing nervously at his wife.

Emily grabbed his hand and held on for dear life. "You should meet her," she told the twins. "We think . . . she's —"

"My aunt!" Ileana appeared beside them. "By the way, stupendous blowout."

"Utterly magical," Miranda agreed. She reached out and took Cam's hand, which had been coiled around the rosemary and valerian root. Taking the herbs, Miranda turned back to Emily and Dave. "Your garden is lovely. Perhaps you could show me around it sometime. I'm very interested in herbs —"

Cam got it!

Recite the Lethe incantation with me, she urged Alex, as their birth mother showed the powerful herb for forgetfulness to Emily, who, as Miranda had known she would, picked it up to examine it, and also handed it to Dave.

A moment later, Emily blinked lazily. "Excuse me," she said to Miranda. "Forgive me. This is terribly embarrassing, but I can't seem to remember your name."

"Miranda," Alex told her happily. "She's Brice Stanley's date's aunt."

"Oh." Emily's smile was warm. "Of course," she said. "How silly of me."

As Ileana and Miranda strolled away, Cam rushed into Emily's and Dave's arms. The family who had reared her had just met the family that she and Alex had been born into, though her adoptive parents had already forgotten. "Tonight is beyond special," she whispered to Dave and Emily.

"Thank you," Alex said, her smile huge, her voice breaking, as, for the second time that night, she piled onto the hugging trio. "We'll never forget all you did for us."

It was nearly midnight when Cam slipped away from the party. She wandered out the front door, where she gathered her robes and settled on the front steps.

Overwhelmed was not a favorite stop on the CAm-trak express, and she'd passed that station hours ago. She needed a quiet moment now and took it to inhale the crisp air of a perfect fall New England night. And to let the events of the past month now whirling in her head settle into some order she could deal with.

She looked up at the sky. There was a full moon tonight. And soon it would be joined by a pink strip of dawn. Sun and moon would share the sky.

Instinctively, she clasped her charm, zipping it slowly back and forth on its chain, the hammered-gold amulet so like her sister's.

Music wafted over the fence from the dual tents out back.

Two parties, Cam was thinking. Two families, two futures . . . Tonight it had all become one.

She sensed Alex coming before she actually heard her sister's footsteps or felt the hand on her shoulder. There was nothing they needed to say to each other, aloud or telepathically.

They could think their separate thoughts, Alex mused, as she sat down beside her sister, separate thoughts that were probably as identical as they were.

Neither of them had imagined in her wildest dreams that Emily and Dave could have accomplished all this.

What they'd proved, though the loving couple probably hadn't even meant to, was how well they knew both their daughters, and how much they loved them both. Dave and Em weren't witches. They had no special powers. But reading human hearts, that was real magick.

And by welcoming Miranda and Ileana, Dave and Emily had given the twins the most treasured gift of all: the permission to be what they were. Daughters of two families, finally together. Twins. Witches. T'Witches.

Only one thing overshadowed the importance of all that. "Yo, birthday girls!" Dylan called from inside the house. "Come on in, dudes. Let's do cake!"

ABOUT THE AUTHORS

H.B. Gilmour is the author of numerous bestselling books for adults and young readers, including the *Clueless* movie novelization and series; *Pretty in Pink,* a University of Iowa Best Book for Young Readers; and *Godzilla,* a Nickelodeon Kids Choice nominee. She also cowrote the award-winning screenplay *Tag.*

H.B. lives in upstate New York with her husband, John Johann, and their misunderstood dog, Fred, one of the family's five pitbulls, three cats, two snakes (a boa constrictor and a python), and five extremely bright, animal-loving children.

Randi Reisfeld has written many bestsellers, such as the *Clueless* series (which she wrote with H.B.); the *Moesha* series; and biographies of Prince William, New Kids on the Block, and Hanson. Her Scholastic paperback *Got Issues Much?* was named an ALA Best Book For Reluctant Readers in 1999.

Randi has always been fascinated with the randomness of life. . . . About how any of our lives can simply "turn on a dime" and instantly (*snap!*) be forever changed. About the power each one of us has deep inside, if only we knew how to access it. About how any of us would react if, out of the blue, we came face-to-face with our exact double.

From those random fascinations, T*Witches was born.

Oh, and BTW: She has no twin (that she knows of) but an extremely cool family and a cadre of BFFs to whom she is totally devoted.

HAVE YOU READ ALL THE BOOKS IN THE
T☉WITCHES SERIES?

T☉WITCHES #1: *THE POWER OF TWO*

Identical twins. Separated at birth. For one very good reason . . .

If they ever met, they could combine their powerful gifts and help people, maybe even save a life. They could figure out who they really are and who their parents really are — or were. And they could fall into very evil hands. Guess what? They're about to meet.

T☉WITCHES #2: *BUILDING A MYSTERY*

Alex and Cam finally learn some secrets about their past. But they still have a lot to uncover. Fortunately, there's new eye candy in town to keep the girls' minds off their troubles. Cade is dark and beautiful and seems to have secrets of his own. Alex is lured in . . . and it takes both girls to break his spell. But are they strong enough to hold back the evil that surrounds them?

ꙮWITCHES #3: *SEEING IS DECEIVING*

Cam's and Alex's powers are getting in sync, and the twins can't help themselves. They're reading people's minds, using magick on the soccer field. It's bringing them closer together. But it's forcing Cam and her bff, Beth, apart.

When Alex sneaks out to an all-night party, she suddenly finds Beth — and herself — in terrible danger. Thantos, the evil one who wants the twins eliminated, has taken Beth hostage. Must Alex sacrifice herself to save her sister and her friend?

ꙮWITCHES #4: *DEAD WRONG*

Alex's skeevy stepdad has resurfaced . . . and he wants Alex back. Like, for good. And Evan, Alex's Montana bud, is crashing. He needs help, stat. Time to 180 to Alex's hometown.

But there's more trouble in Montana than the twins ever expected. The powerful warlock Thantos has followed Cam and Alex. And he has a present for them. One that's six feet under.

T◉WITCHES #5: *DON'T THINK TWICE*

Cam's best, Bree, is unraveling, and Cam feels locked out. Not so for Alex, who has been breaking into people's minds. She knows all Bree's secrets. But before the twins can help Bree, she is taken away. To a private place, for serious help.

There, Bree meets a mysterious woman who is able to heal her like no one else. But this woman is more than a stranger. She holds the key to everything that Cam and Alex have been searching for. If only they can get to her.

T◉WITCHES #6: *DOUBLE JEOPARDY*

Miranda. The mother Cam and Alex never knew they had. A magnificent witch from the most powerful family on Coventry Island.

Rewind.

Locked away in a sanitarium the twins' whole lives, Miranda is broken. Physically and spiritually. And her freedom comes with a price. Cam and Alex will have to part with something that means more to them than they ever imagined.

And for once, their guardians can't help them.

T☉WITCHES #7: *KINDRED SPIRITS*

Coventry Island. A lush, hidden world of magick and sorcery. It's where Cam and Alex were born. And it's where they're headed now. But Coventry doesn't feel much like home. A group of cooler-than-thou teen witches and warlocks aren't exactly making nice with the twins. And if Cam and Alex feel like the odd girls out in this place . . . where is it that they *really* belong?

T☉WITCHES #8: *THE WITCH HUNTERS*

Cam and Alex are back in Marble Bay, but nothing's back to normal. Their bffs are being way weird. And there's a creepy character in town who is definitely not down with anything witchy. This baddie is *serious* about putting a stop to sorcery and magick. And that means the twins.

T☉WITCHES #9: *SPLIT DECISION*

It's summer. And for the first time since they've met, Cam and Alex are doing their own things. Alex is chilling in Marble Bay with her sweetie, Cade. And Cam is in Coventry with her warlock hottie, Shane. But the twins don't realize that when they're apart, their magick is weakened — making them easy prey for wicked forces. And suddenly evil is everywhere.